FLYING UP T

FLYING UP THE MOUNTAIN

Elizabeth-Irene Baitie

ACCORD BOOKS

Norton Young Readers

An Imprint of W. W. Norton & Company
Celebrating a Century of Independent Publishing

To my readers, who make it all worthwhile.

For information about permission to reproduce selections from this book, write to Permissions, W. W. Norton & Company, Inc., 500 Fifth Avenue, New York, NY 10110

For information about special discounts for bulk purchases, please contact W. W. Norton Special Sales at specialsales@wwnorton.com or 800-233-4830

Manufacturing by Lakeside Book Company
Book design by Beth Steidle and Hana Anouk Nakamura
Production manager: Delaney Adams

ISBN 978-1-324-05267-8

W. W. Norton & Company, Inc., 500 Fifth Avenue, New York, N.Y. 10110
www.wwnorton.com

W. W. Norton & Company Ltd., 15 Carlisle Street, London W1D 3BS

1 2 3 4 5 6 7 8 9 0

FLYING UP THE MOUNTAIN

CHAPTER ONE

THE PEREGRINE FALCON TIGHTENED HIS GRIP ON THE branch up in the neem tree.

It was unusual, he thought to himself; a prize falcon lurking in a garden tree. But he figured it was just the sort of thing one would expect in this garden. After all, it was a magical enough place, with herbs, bark, flowers, leaves, and roots that could be used for everything from healing sprained ankles to making tasty salads. He grimaced as he remembered the bitter taste of neem steam. Months earlier, it had cured him of a raging fever.

The falcon's binocular eyes locked onto its target: She stood on the front porch of her house. Her back was to the garden. Her phone to her ear. Despite his good hearing, the falcon couldn't pick up her words. She was too far away.

He smiled cunningly. It was time to pounce on his target. Nothing could escape a falcon in its stoop. By the time she sensed him coming, it would be too late.

He hopped down from the tree and plucked up a small bunch of flowers from where they grew along the wall in red, pink, and yellow blooms. Then he began his approach: Awful speed. Deadly silence. The falcon could usually see his hapless victim from a mile away—while it was still oblivious to the deadly predator plummeting toward it. He clenched his foot, ready to strike the mortal blow that would stun his prey. He was within a few feet. Now he could hear her.

"Nnoma's secret?" Nana said into her phone, giving an ironic chuckle. "If I knew anything and I told you, it would no longer be a secret, would it?"

Ato paused. He was no longer a falcon in lethal attack. Now he was in his twelve-year-old boy's body, and all ears. A secret on Nnoma? Who was his grandmother talking to?

There was silence. Nana was listening to the other person. "Do I think anyone else out there knows anything?" she asked. Her voice was sober. "Eyra does. You and I both know that."

Eyra. The mysterious owner of Nnoma, the bird island he was going to tomorrow.

Ato knew he wasn't meant to eavesdrop. Time to fly, he thought, fast as a falcon. He took a step back. Too late. His grandmother had caught sight of his movement. She whipped her head around. Her frown vanished. Affection lit up her face.

"Your partner is out of the tree now," she exclaimed into the phone, in a lighter voice. She spread out her arms invitingly to Ato. "Come, dear!"

"For you, Nana," the falcon mumbled. He thrust out his bunched fist.

His grandmother took the flowers, cooing her pleasure.

She handed him her cell phone and dropped a kiss on his sweaty forehead.

"Here, talk to your friend while I go get our lunch ready."

Ato put the phone to his ear.

"Hi, kiddo!"

"Max!" Ato broke into a smile on hearing the man's brisk, friendly tone. Ever since Max had helped him nail the Prophet of Fire, he and the skinny reporter had become buddies.

"Wanted to say a quick 'bye before you set off," Max said. "I called your mum. She said you were with your grandmother. Boy, you must be as ready as a preacher on Sunday morning!"

Ato's smile widened even farther. "I've waited my whole life for this."

"Ha, ha. Five out of your twelve years is hardly all your life. Have mega-fun, Ato!"

Ato glanced furtively behind him. He dropped his voice.

"Max. What were you and Nana talking about? I heard her say something about a secret."

There was a brief pause. Then Max laughed. "I thought you were up in a tree!"

"I was. I was doing a falcon stoop. Nana didn't hear me coming," he said proudly.

Max chuckled. "You might need a falcon's eyes and hearing when you get to Nnoma. Perhaps I've been wearing my investigative cap too tightly, but I keep wondering why Nnoma's been closed for so long. Five years. Could there be some hidden reason? I asked your nana. No joy. But something doesn't add up. To me, at least."

Ato shrugged. This was just Max being Max. The most important thing for him now was that Nnoma was finally open. "It doesn't matter anymore, Max."

"I hope that's true, Ato. I really do."

✦✦✦✦✦✦✦

That night, Ato lay in bed with the sweetness of Nana's fried plantain lingering at the back of his throat. This was his last sleepover at his grandmother's before the four-hour drive to the ferry that would take him and his friends to Nnoma the next day. He wriggled beneath his sheet in delight. For five years he'd dreamt of going to Nnoma, the famous island, the nature paradise where thousands of bird species lived protected. His father had helped to make it a sanctuary that children could visit. Now he and his friends were finally getting to go there: his dream had come true!

His mind traveled back a few months, when his hopes of going to Nnoma had been shattered. He and his friends had designed a project that they'd hoped would get them to the island. But some cruel person had burned their project to ashes, and had poisoned a beautiful nature pond so he could steal farmland nearby. To think the brain behind this evil act was the most powerful man in Ato's community—the Prophet of Fire! Facing him had been scary, but thanks to Nana, Ato had put his fear aside. Max had helped him too. Soon he and his friends had exposed the Prophet for what he really was: A ruthless man who would destroy anything—and anyone—to get what he wanted. A man who even made children in an orphanage suffer so he could get rich. Now the Prophet was behind bars. Ato sighed happily at the thought. His community was safe again.

Too excited to sleep, he sat up and switched on his bedside lamp. He reached into the backpack on the floor beside him. His fingers closed around a piece of paper softened from having been folded and unfolded hundreds of times. He read the bold slant of his father's handwriting:

My son, it's been months of hard work, but now the dream is forming before my eyes. I'm sitting at the highest point of Nnoma: It's called the Dawn Locus. One day I hope you will sit here with me. Ato, now that the Nnoma dream is here, it must stay alive. Those of us who believe in it must protect it. For now, the sun shines, but enemy storms are gathering. One day they may be unleashed. If they are, I have a plan. It is protected, somewhere below this rock peak, where the sunlight first greets Nnoma, where the falcons watch over the valley. Whenever I hold you in my arms, I can see you are truly like me—Asafo, a protector of our world. When your steps are strong enough to match mine, we shall walk this mountainside together, to protect this dream. Only a few people are privileged enough to step on Nnoma. You will be one of them. You'll prove yourself good enough to come here. I've asked Mummy to blow on your little toes to make you laugh. One day, your toes will be firm enough to grip this rock.

Ato flung himself back on the bed, dizzy with happiness. He was going to be an Asafo! Was his father proud of him all the way up in heaven? he wondered.

For years, two questions had lurked in his head: What were the enemy storms his father had written about? And what exactly was his father's plan? The bedside lamp threw soft yellow light onto the ceiling. A familiar pair of eyes glinted down at him, sharp and intelligent.

"I wish I could see and hear like you can," he whispered up at them.

The peregrine falcon did not answer. It was painted onto his ceiling. Its outspread wings covered half the white space. Ato ran an admiring gaze over the barred pattern on its chest. Falcons were his absolute favorite birds. Fast, clever, and ever so deadly, and with eyes that could see objects from a mile away. They hunted down their targets with deadly accuracy. That's what he needed. Speed. Accuracy. He carefully refolded the only letter he had from his father and tucked it back into his bag.

His door swung open. Nana padded in, a mug between her cupped hands.

"Just as I thought—you're still up. Here's a nightcap, darling. I don't want the excitement to keep you awake."

His tongue twitched. He was dying to ask about the secret she'd mentioned on the phone. But his mother had often reprimanded him for listening in on other people's conversations. So he swallowed his curiosity. Instead, he took the warm mug, snuggled into her good-night cuddle, and breathed in the fragrant steam from her passionflower, honey, and lavender brew. He took a small sip. The evil man had been locked away. And Ato was going to Nnoma. Everything was fine. He sighed as Nana whispered prayers above his head, for protection and happiness on Nnoma. Minutes later, she took the mug from his still hands as he drifted into sleep, still smiling.

CHAPTER TWO

THE FOLLOWING DAY, ATO STOOD IN THE LINE OF KIDS WITH his two best friends, Leslie and Dzifa. All sixty-four children had lined up on the wooden pier at the edge of the Volta Lake. Its rippling surface reflected the August afternoon sunshine.

"Lots of kids from lots of countries," Ato remarked.

"Like a bag of mixed candies," Leslie agreed.

Ato noticed that Leslie looked bulkier than normal today in his baggy cabin pants with multiple zippered pockets.

The swarm of parents and guardians had long gone, with their endless goodbyes and moist eyes. *Arrive only with the clothes and shoes you are wearing*, their invitation letter to Nnoma had instructed. Yet Ato had seen dozens of parents having to reluctantly lug back huge pull-along cases they'd packed for their kids. Leslie's mum had driven off with three bulging lunch packs.

Ato looked eagerly at the ferry. It was moored to the pier with ropes as thick as his arm. A metal gangway sloped toward them. Sixteen men and women, eight each, lined the gangway. They had introduced themselves as Guardians. On the front of their blue

T-shirts were their names: KAI, RICHIE, FRANK, SOWAH, JONES, KOKU, BEA, CHRISTIAN, PEACE, HAMID, ARABA . . . Some looked like friendly older brothers and sisters. A few looked more like no-nonsense teachers. Frank was hulking and hairy. "Frank the Tank," Dzifa whispered. Ato stifled a laugh. It was true. Frank looked as if he could sink the ferry with one stomp of his foot on the deck.

A tall Guardian with cornrows stepped forward and gestured for silence. She had broad shoulders, tight lips, and bulging eyes. KAI, her T-shirt read. Her eyeballs swiveled in their sockets, regarding them as if she wanted them cross-legged on the floor with a finger on their lips, nursery-school-style.

"Welcome aboard, Flock Eleven."

Ato winced. Her voice was thin and tense, scratching the air like squeaky glass.

At once, a huge white banner unfurled on the deck of the ferry. FLOCK ELEVEN, AKWAABA, it proclaimed.

The gathered kids cheered and Ato's heart leapt. This was truly happening! He was going to become an Asafo!

"Flock Eleven," she continued. "You are the eleventh set of young people to visit our beautiful island of Nnoma since it opened ten years ago. We, your Guardians, are one hundred percent responsible for you while you are on Nnoma. And you, Flock Eleven, will be one hundred percent obedient to us." Kai's eyes were stern and humorless, set in a face that demanded good behavior from children two hundred percent of the time. She scanned them continuously and suspiciously. Maybe she expected one of them to dive off the gangway into the lake, Ato thought.

Ato turned around. "We don't want to cross *her*," he whispered to his friends.

"If we behave ourselves, we won't to have to worry about that," Leslie said piously.

Dzifa grimaced. "Some people don't need crossing. They're always cross."

A beefy Guardian stepped up. He was over six feet tall with a dark, muscular body that glistened with perspiration. RICHIE, his T-shirt read. Eyes twinkling, he beckoned them up the gangway. The line started to inch forward slowly and the waiting kids began whispered conversations about the owner of Nnoma: Eyra. Ato knew she was hardly ever seen beyond the island, and rarely spoke to the media. One kid had heard that she lived high up the island in a cabin surrounded by woods.

"She lives in a cave," said another girl, with certainty.

"I bet she wears a skirt made from leaves. Like Eve in the Bible," Leslie added.

There were more guesses about Eyra: That she walked barefoot everywhere and swung from trees like Jane of the Jungle. And that she ate locusts and honey, like John the Baptist. One boy was sure Eyra only used sign language and birdcalls.

After several minutes of this speculation, Ato and his friends were still only halfway down the line of impatient kids.

"What is this, the Tortoise Express?" Dzifa muttered, craning her neck. She only stood as high as Ato's ears.

Ato knew how much Dzifa hated waiting for anything.

"There's some kind of security check," he said, peering ahead.

Leslie frowned. "A check? Why?"

"For stuff they don't want on Nnoma, I guess," said a little voice behind them.

Ato turned to see a girl about his height, with her hair bunched in two fluffy black puffs. She had small, sad eyes.

"You're right," he said to her. He could see clearer now. Just beyond the gangway, there was a narrow hall with hundreds of small square slats along both walls. The slats were covered in dark mesh, and were each the size of a mobile phone. Ato noticed that as kids made their way through the walkway, a bright yellow light would occasionally flash in all the slats. Every time this happened, a Guardian would search through a child's pockets and take out something. Wrapped sweets. A pack of cookies. A plastic bottled drink. Plastic toys.

Richie the Guardian smiled at Ato and his friends as they drew closer to him. Ato peered curiously through the slats.

"Those are bees!" the girl with sad eyes exclaimed.

Richie raised his eyebrows, looking impressed. "Good observation, Hafsat!" he remarked.

"Bees? How does that work, Richie?" Ato asked in surprise.

"Like body-scan machines. Or sniffer dogs. These little fellas do the same thing. Three thousand of them. They detect stuff we *don't* want on Nnoma. Harmful substances. Plastics. Dangerous chemicals. Insecticides. No protection is too much for Nnoma. After their security side hustle here, we return them to the hive to continue their day jobs—pollination and making honey. Easy."

Leslie shrank back, but Ato nudged him forward. It was like

trying to shove a tree. Ato knew Leslie kept a careful distance from tiny critters—ants, wasps, bugs, germs.

"Come on." Richie urged them forward. "These bees are on the same side as us—Team Nnoma."

It turned out that Leslie had good reason to hang back. The sensor lights blinked furiously when he finally shuffled past.

"Sorry," Richie said, fishing out three mini-cans of bug spray from Leslie's zippered pants pockets. "This is like nerve gas for our insects on Nnoma. And birds eat insects. So stuff that's toxic to insects ends up being toxic to birds."

The Guardian dropped the cans purposefully into a large bag hanging from a wall hook. "Bees have a super-smart sense of smell," he explained, with a sympathetic pat on Leslie's shoulder. "These are trained to recognize certain smells. Plastics. Pollutants. Chemicals. We give them sugar water when those substances are around. Pretty soon every time they smell them, they stick out their tongues expecting a shot of the sweet stuff. When enough of them stick out their tongues, it sets off the sensor lights. Pretty amazing stuff. That way nothing gets here that would harm any animal, plant, or person on Nnoma. Everything on this island is protected."

Deprived of his arsenal, Leslie eyed the lake gloomily while Richie relieved another boy of a plastic toy gun. "We're going into a jungle with nothing to protect *us*," Leslie muttered to his friends. "This trip is going to be one hundred percent nightmare."

Ato turned to his friend. If there was anyone who could talk about how badly things could turn out, it was Leslie.

"C'mon," he said reassuringly, "Nnoma is gonna be one hundred percent awesome."

Leslie muttered something about Ato's foolishness, and one by one they had their pictures taken under the Akwaaba banner. Snapshots done, the three friends finally stepped into the main hall of the vessel. The hall had glass windows all around with spectacular three-sixty views of the lake, which glowed orange from the setting sun. Inside, the hall was decked for a party. Colored streamers, banners, and welcome posters stretched from one end of it to the other. Several glass tables laden with strange new foods and circled with red leather chairs invited them to feast.

And feast they did, although the girl who'd made the correct guess about the bees was so slow to choose her food that she held everyone up the dinner queue for several minutes—and then picked out a single knobbly purple fruit.

Over dinner and music and games, Ato got to meet the kids he would be spending the next seven days with. There were kids with strange accents. Kids who acted as if they'd been raised on the ferry. Those who cracked jokes every second. Shy ones biting their nails. Solemn ones who stared at everyone in silence. Braggarts going on nonstop about their projects. Dance-floor show-offs. Girls who chewed gum and played with their braids. Curious ones who wouldn't stop asking questions, and a tall boy with bushy eyebrows called Bello who had answers to everyone's questions.

After dinner, the Guardians showed a video. Ato watched, enthralled, as Asafo spoke about what they were doing. From their "before" pictures on the deck of the ferry, he could see they had once looked just like he did now, grinning under the AKWAABA banner. Now they were taller. They spoke with squared shoulders and steady gazes. They feared no one: not powerful people old enough to be their parents, nor crooked politicians and presidents of large companies, nor community leaders with greedy eyes who looked like they could swallow Asafo for a snack. And the Asafo were making them change things. Beaches got cleaner, vulnerable animals were protected, waters cleared up, and factories became safer.

Asafo: Speaking truth to power, read the caption at the top of the screen.

The lights in the hall came on. The kids sat in silent admiration for a few seconds.

"Isn't it awesome! They *are* changing the world," Dzifa breathed to Ato.

"They're so brave," Leslie said humbly.

Ato tapped Leslie's hand. "We're brave too. Remember, we exposed the Prophet."

"I can't wait to become an Asafo!" a squeaky-voiced boy announced. A chuckle went around the room and the Guardians lined up in front.

"Let me explain one thing to you," Richie said. "All of you are going to Nnoma. But not all of you will become Asafo."

Ato's hands dropped to his side. What on earth did Richie mean? Murmurs of surprise and protest went around the hall.

"But I thought we were all going to be Asafo!" the tall boy, Bello, declared.

"That's not fair!" someone exclaimed.

"Being an Asafo is a tough job," Kai said. "It means putting others before yourself. It means speaking up even when you're afraid."

"So who gets chosen?" Ato asked, trying to keep the worry out of his voice.

"You'll find out, after we get to the island. After you meet Eyra. She's excited to see you."

Ato's heart fluttered. Eyra. Did she know his father? he wondered.

Shortly afterward the Guardians began a set of games, and the hall was once again ringing with fun and laughter.

♦ ♦ ♦ ♦ ♦ ♦

Much later that night, Ato could not sleep. He lay on his back on the upper bunk staring out the porthole into the jeweled night sky. The thrill of the games was over. The ferry was gliding slowly and silently toward Nnoma. In his cabin, Leslie and two other boys were breathing slowly in their bunks, deep in sleep. He had been so sure he would be an Asafo. There were sixty-four children. Would he be chosen? He had hoped for so long to become an Asafo. And to find his father's plan. Please, God, he mouthed silently. Please.

CHAPTER THREE

ATO'S HANDS CLENCHED THE COOL RAILS OF THE FERRY. THE vessel glided to the edge of the gray water. It was the next morning, and ahead, rising from the lake, was Nnoma. It looked so peaceful, minding its own business, just being an island, he thought. What enemies could it have? The tropical island was green and hilly, its lower slopes thick with trees. Higher up and farther east, rocks and dense shrubs took over. Ato's eyes traveled up toward the highest point of the island—the Dawn Locus. A crown of morning mist circled it, like a ghostly veil.

Please, God, he prayed again. Could that be where his father had kept his plan? Was it still there?

Dzifa's eyes danced in her pixie face. "We're finally here!"

Ato allowed himself a smile.

"Cheer up," Dzifa said firmly, reading his mind. "We'll get to be Asafo. And we'll find your dad's plan. I know we will."

Her words comforted him. She always sounded as if she could get whatever she wanted. He liked that about her.

Leslie eyed the chattering kids crowded along the ferry rails. "That's what everyone here thinks."

"Leslie, Ato." Dzifa spoke in a steely voice that Ato called her magpie tone. She slipped her arms through theirs, linking them all together. "You can't give up before we've even started! Now, let's have a *winner's* attitude. The three of us are a great team. Look what we did to make it here, even after our project got burned down!"

Leslie squinted at the island and the surrounding water. "About that plan, though, Ato. Do you think it will still be here? After ten years?"

"My father wrote in his letter that it was protected."

"Ten years in this place is a long time," Leslie said ominously.

Bello moved up the rails, close to them.

"Hello, Bello," Dzifa said. "Must be nice to be able to make rhymes with your name."

"Oh yeah. Hello, Bello, my good fellow, looking mellow, playin' that cello," he sang. His bushy black eyebrows twitched up and down like twin caterpillars as he swung his arms rapper-style.

A flock of black-and-white birds flapped past the ferry, honking raucously and interrupting Bello.

"Hornbills!" Ato exclaimed, recognizing the birds by their thick, long beaks. "I saw them when my grandma took me on a trip to the river. There aren't as many of them around now, though. She said it's 'cos the old trees they live in are all being chopped down for timber."

"You have a smart grandmother," Richie remarked, coming up behind them.

Ato nodded with pride. As the ferry slowed to a stop, Ato's eyes widened, taking in the vividly colored flocks: white waders at the water's edge, gray speckled birds with long beaks on the shores, green birds with blue-tinged feathers flitting low past the ferry . . .

"Hundreds of species of birds gather on Nnoma at different times of the year," Richie said to the entranced children. He pointed out tiny orange-and-purple pygmy kingfishers, bright-yellow-and-green weaverbirds, white-faced ducks, and golden orioles.

Ato felt his chest puff up like a pigeon's. How he wanted to tell them that his father had helped to make this island a paradise that children could visit!

A powerful bird swooped across the surface of the lake. There was a collective gasp from the deck as it rose again, its wide wings beating the air. In its talons was a large wriggling fish.

Ato recognized it at once. "That's an African fish eagle!" he exclaimed. The kids around him looked impressed and he struggled to hide his smile.

"The eagle: king of all birds," Bello declared.

"For me, the king is the fastest hunter of them all—the peregrine falcon!" Ato replied.

Bello's caterpillar eyebrows jerked up together. He looked like a sixth-grade teacher who'd discovered a child in his class who couldn't read. "You think a falcon could beat an eagle? You've got some learning to do. When I become an Asafo, I'll make sure kids like you get taught these things properly in school."

"An eagle is bigger and stronger. But it could never catch a peregrine falcon. And that's what counts . . ." Ato began explaining.

But Bello wasn't listening. Another bird had caught his attention.

Ato forced himself not to look annoyed at being called "kid." Just because Bello was taller than everyone else, he was acting big and all. A falcon was king in *his* opinion, he told himself. He'd heard people say you could be reborn in another life and come back as an animal. If that was true, next time he came back to earth he wanted to be a peregrine falcon. To look as fearsome as the one on the ceiling of his bedroom in Nana's house. He eyed Bello and imagined the thrill of swooping down on him at blinding speed.

The voices around him dropped to a hush. The mist had broken. Nnoma's peak, the Dawn Locus, was now fully in view. Sunshine burst off the towering rock face, radiating golden beams in every direction. It looked like the gleam of a prize, he thought.

Hafsat, or the Bee-Spotter, as he had secretly nicknamed her, turned to him. Something glinted in her eyes. Was that a tear? he wondered. Or a reflection of the sky?

She brushed a hand across her eyes. "Nnoma looks so beautiful. Do you know why it was closed for so long?" she asked him.

Ato shook his head. Max too had asked the same question. On impulse, he tapped a Guardian, standing with her back to him. She turned. At once, he regretted his action. It was Kai.

"Yes, Ato?"

"I just wondered, Kai. Why has Nnoma been closed all those years?"

Her eyes pinned him down, cool as marbles. "It's open now, isn't it?" she said stiffly. Then she was striding away toward the front of the ferry.

Ato looked after her. Nnoma was meant to be open—for children to understand birds and wildlife and nature, and to become Asafo. He suddenly realized that, like Max, he *did* want to know why the paradise his father had helped to develop had been closed for so long.

CHAPTER FOUR

EYRA WAS WAITING FOR THEM ON THE SHORE, WITH A FLOWY white dress and a huge smile of welcome. She was a tall lady, slender as a reed, with a cloud of black hair that framed her face like a dark halo.

She raised her arms, sleeves billowing like a swan's wings at takeoff. "Flock Eleven, I've waited five years to see you, and here you are!" Her voice was throaty, deep, and strong. It sent an electric thrill down Ato's spine. As the Guardians led them in a line toward her, he took in her commanding face, with high cheekbones and magnetic black eyes.

With a smile and a hug, she welcomed each child one by one, congratulating them on their winning entry projects, asking questions about the ferry ride, and sounding like an auntie they had known their whole lives.

"She knows everyone's name!" Dzifa whispered.

As Ato stepped up to her, her warm eyes met his and her smile widened. When she embraced him, he breathed in lemongrass and flowers.

"Welcome, Ekow's son," she murmured in a voice so low that only he could hear her. Still holding him, she whispered against his ear, "I know he's proud of you right now, and I am *overjoyed* to have you here. The world needs you, young warrior."

His head spun at her words. A warrior, she called him! She let go of him and he stumbled on unsteadily. She remembered his father! She knew who he was! He felt dazed with joy, his feet floating above the ground.

"Hey, earth to Ato, earth to Ato!" Dzifa teased, drawing abreast of him. "She recognized you, didn't she!"

He nodded, dizzy with pleasure, and sat on the grass with everyone else, waiting for Eyra to finish welcoming them all.

When she was done, Eyra turned to them, her forehead glistening with light perspiration.

"Flock Eleven," she said, "you're here for seven days. In this precious time, it's going to be just you, your Guardians, and me. At the end of this period, some of you will become Asafo, and some will be Friends. Whether you become Asafo or Friends, the earth is going to need you; that's what your seven days here are preparing you for. But first, it's time for you to get some food!" She hung behind watching as the Guardians took over. Richie led Flock Eleven up a dirt path that cut through the green hillside, away from the ferry. To Ato, the voices of Flock Eleven competed squarely with the twittering and shrilling of a thousand island birds.

Soon a dome-shaped building with a flat top came into view in a clearing ahead of them. Richie pointed to it. "That's the Pecking

Bowl—where we eat. First one there grabs the best seat!" he said with a laugh.

"Last one there's a loon!" Dzifa called, looking at Bello. She took off like a jet, black braids flying behind her, with Bello, Leslie, and a horde of other kids on her heels.

I'm not racing against Professor Bello, Ato thought peevishly. A shadow fell beside him. It was Hafsat. She smiled at him, warmth slipping into her sad eyes. "Isn't that Pecking Bowl beautiful?" she asked, pointing at it.

Ato agreed. The building had giant arching bamboo beams that curved from its roof to the ground. It felt like they were standing in front of a massive, upside-down bird-feeding bowl.

Inside, he and Hafsat joined Dzifa and Leslie at their table. Bello and three other kids sat with them, all marveling at the huge circular hall. Along its curved walls, wooden trestles were laden with food: fruits of all kinds, a rainbow of vegetables, steaming clay pots of porridge, and a selection of breads.

"No bananas?" Leslie asked Richie, who had just come up behind them.

"Don't expect to recognize more than a few foods here," the tall Guardian said with a wink.

Ato did recognize a couple of fruits that he'd tried when Nana had taken him on a day trip to a farm three hours away from home. One was a deep purple fruit shaped like a pebble. It was sweet and pulpy and had turned his tongue and teeth black. Then there were the tart little berries that looked like tiny orange eggs. Everything else was new to him.

Rows of earthenware pots bubbled with milled black rice and tigernut porridge, fragrant sorghum porridge, and spicy millet porridge. An array of bread and cakes baked from ancient grains, served with nut butters and wild honey, tempted Ato. There were also bean sauces, wild yams, roasted plantain, and nut biscuits. Ato eventually chose a sorghum-and-peanut porridge with bean cakes. He also served himself some unusual fruit. It helped that they'd all been labeled—cashew apples, stewed noni, and sisibi, which looked almost exactly like a cluster of grapes.

"Hopefully these won't give me a tummy ache," Leslie said doubtfully. Then he proceeded to help himself to a bowl of porridge, two cashew apples, a scoop of creamy atemoya from its lumpy fruit case, and two helpings of soursop from within its spiky skin. "Tastes like custard," he declared, and promptly took a third helping of soursop.

"May I have some sugar in my porridge?" he asked Richie, who had settled at the head of their table.

Richie pointed to a wooden bowl in the center of their table. It was packed with small red berries. "Try one of those," he said. "After that, taste your porridge."

Ato recognized them. Nana had them growing in bright red clusters on a bush in her garden. "Taami," he exclaimed, and popped a couple of the oval-shaped berries into his mouth.

Leslie cautiously sucked a berry, then spooned his porridge into his mouth. He raised his brows in happy surprise. "My porridge tastes sweet!"

"I eat them all the time at Nana's," Ato bragged. "Even lemons taste sweet after these."

Richie sat down at the head of their table, with an arm over the back of his chair. "Everyone in the world gobbles the same old rice, corn, wheat, and potatoes," he said. "But there are so many other superfoods, like these. They make us healthy and strong, and still protect the earth. A pity not enough people eat them."

Dzifa nodded her agreement.

The talk at the table soon turned to their projects. All the kids here had the best projects from across West Africa, Richie reminded them.

Bello was quick to tell them about the green household cleaner he'd made, and how everyone in his community had begun using it. He'd also visited dozens of schools to teach kids how to make it, he finished, biting into a bean cake.

"That *is* impressive," Dzifa agreed.

He nodded. "When I become an Asafo, the whole world will learn about my good ideas."

Ato exchanged a *who does he think he is?* look with Leslie, and turned to Hafsat. "What did you do?" he asked her.

Her eyes lit up. "I wrote a recipe book—cooking with plants and herbs that are around us. We shouldn't be flying in food from far-off places, it's bad for the environment. My book showed that we can grow so much right here. It was featured in the newspapers."

"Did you get help with your project?" A note of challenge crept into Bello's voice.

She lowered her eyes. "My . . . my dad helped me."

"I did mine by myself," Bello said. He flicked an imaginary fly from his shoulder and turned to Ato.

"How did your project change your community, Ato?" His eyes were cool and questioning.

"Umm . . ." Ato began. He wasn't sure where to start, seeing that their actual project had been burned to cinders by the Prophet of Fire.

Dzifa stepped in. "We gave dozens of kids a chance for a better future. And we helped a farmer get his land back from someone who was trying to steal it. It's a long story. But it was all on Sunshine TV."

Hafsat started at the mention of Sunshine TV. It was a small movement, but Ato caught it.

Bello arched a bushy black eyebrow in approval. "The biggest TV station in Ghana! I'm looking at you with respect now."

"You should." Dzifa smiled smugly.

Now, Ato fumed inwardly.

Bello's serious voice carried across the table. "Richie, it must have cost a lot of money to build the children's camp on Nnoma. And we don't pay to come here. So where does the money come from?"

Richie lowered his fork. "That's a good question. Eyra has enough money. And people around the world who believe in Nnoma donate money to preserve the island." He frowned slightly. "People do wonder, not me of course, other people . . . they wonder what will happen when the money runs out."

Kai was walking behind their table. She caught Richie's words, stopped short, and flashed him a disapproving look. "Nnoma will *always* have enough money, Richie," she said in a tight voice. "Now let's get these kids to their cabins."

Ato jumped up. He couldn't wait to see where they'd be sleeping. And to get a few minutes away from that annoying Bello.

CHAPTER FIVE

ATO JOINED FLOCK ELEVEN, FOLLOWING RICHIE, KAI, AND several other Guardians along a path that wound up the green hillside and into the forest. A large wooden sign that read CABINSIDE was nailed to the trunk of one of the trees at the edge of the woods. As they skipped past it, Hafsat stopped to examine a plant with pretty, fan-shaped leaves. Kai turned around and brusquely called her back in line. Hafsat straightened up and hurried over to join them.

"My dad grows . . . grew these in our garden back home," she said to Ato. "Just outside my bedroom window."

"You should meet my nana," he replied, smiling. "She loves plants too."

They were soon within the woods, surrounded by massive trees with sturdy trunks and thick twisting roots. Their leaves blocked off the sun's rays and the air was heavy with the smells of moldering vegetation, damp earth, and sweet wood. Up every tree was a set of rungs nailed to the trunk that led up to a small wooden cabin supported by broad branches. Each cabin was about ten square feet, and complete with roof, windows, and shutters. A raffia mat covered the entrance of each one.

"Flock Eleven, your home for the next seven days!" Richie called with a dramatic sweep of his arms. He and the other Guardians briskly began assigning them to cabins.

"Ato Turkson and Leslie Quaye!" A short, thick Guardian called Koku called out. He pointed to their cabin with an arm the size of a tree trunk. "Change into your Nnoma clothes and be back down in fifteen minutes."

Ato scrambled up the rungs that had been nailed into the wide trunk. Leslie crept up cautiously behind him.

"I bet we'll sleep on the floor on sackcloth. With a grass pillow," Leslie fretted on their way up.

Ato pushed past the woven raffia mat and stepped into the square cabin. Its walls were smooth panels of bright wood that softly reflected light. On the wall to their left was a bunk bed. Across from it, a window opened to a view of the wooded hillside that stretched all the way down to the lake.

"Wow!" Ato gasped.

Leslie entered after him and gazed out the window, impressed into silence.

Ato returned his gaze to the room. An open bamboo closet stood against the wall on the left. On the shelves, clothes had been rolled and stacked like green and blue mini-logs—seven sets of clothes each—and a pair of walking shoes, sandals, and wet shoes each. Their names had been printed across the front of their T-shirts.

"Not bad," Leslie admitted, testing the mattress on the lower bunk. "Soft."

Ato slipped his feet into his sandals. They felt as snug as gloves. "Try them on," he urged Leslie.

But Leslie had thought about something else. His gaze flicked around the room. "Where's the bathroom?" he asked anxiously.

A sliding panel on a far wall revealed the tiny bathroom. Leslie examined a rack beside the shower that held black soap, shea body butter, charcoal toothpaste, and charcoal powder. "All-natural stuff here," he said, reading the labels. "Oh." He sounded sheepish. "There's even insect repellent."

Ato laughed.

A gray shadow flicked across the bottom of the doorway, and a slim gecko scurried across the floor.

"Seven days," Leslie mused. "Seven days in the wild."

"Seven busy days," Ato repeated slowly, his attention drawn to a paper notice pinned behind their door:

> Rise and Shine: 7 a.m.
>
> Breakfast: 7:30–8:30 a.m.
>
> Flocking Valley and/or Missions: 9 a.m.–12 p.m.
>
> Lunch: 12:30–1:30 p.m.
>
> Nest Rest: 2 p.m.–3 p.m.
>
> Flocking Valley and/or Missions: 3:30 p.m.–5:45 p.m.
>
> Dinner: 6 p.m.–7 p.m.
>
> Bedtime: 8 p.m.

"Mission? Flocking Valley?" Leslie asked. "What are those?"

Ato shrugged. "I dunno. But . . ." He eyed the schedule. It looked packed. "I hope I'll have time to spare . . . to look for the plan."

Leslie placed a comforting arm around his shoulder. "I'll help you. But let's face it: this island is pretty big."

It was, Ato thought in agreement. He looked out the window at the shale stone paths that led like lines of puzzle pieces from the cabins, merging into footpaths that stretched all the way to the lake and the towering mountain.

"*Somewhere below this rock peak. Where the falcons watch over the valley*," he said to Leslie. "That's what my dad wrote. I think it's somewhere on the mountain."

"It's a pretty wide mountain," Leslie said in a *don't get your hopes up* tone.

Ato sighed and began to change out of his clothes. Maybe Eyra would know something. At the first chance he got, he would ask her.

◆ ◆ ◆ ◆ ◆ ◆ ◆

At least half of Flock Eleven was already down when Ato descended with Leslie to the forest floor. Everyone was wearing blue-and-green Nnoma T-shirts. It was an attractive sight. Ato smiled: he was really here! he reminded himself. He walked over to Dzifa, who stood beside Bello on a giant tree root. They were both laughing.

"You guys are lucky. You got each other," Dzifa remarked. "I'm sharing with Hafsat. I'd finished changing by the time she climbed up to our cabin."

"And I just told Dzifa her roommate has two speeds. Slow and stop," Bello said. He and Dzifa laughed again, then suddenly he switched his attention.

"By the way, my fellow competitors," he said. "Did you notice our shoes are biodegradable?"

"Competitors?" Ato asked.

Bello shrugged. "Aren't we? Only some of us will get to be Asafo. It's definitely some kind of competition. Anyway, back to our shoes. I think there's sugarcane in them."

"Sugarcane? In *shoes*?" Ato snorted.

Richie had come up behind them. He patted Bello's shoulder. "He's right. The soles are made from both sugarcane and natural rubber."

"Well, *hello*, Bello!" Dzifa smiled.

Ato felt a warm rush of embarrassment. He had sounded dumb. On the island where his father had done such splendid work.

"Good on Nnoma," Bello said to Richie. "'Cos it takes forty years for sneakers to break down. Or more. I'm guessing the leather in the shoes is responsibly sourced? Recycled leather?"

"And following Dzifa, *hello*, Bello!" Richie looked impressed.

Ato saw a look on Dzifa's face. One she rarely gave to anyone: admiration.

Responsibly sourced? Bello sounded like a teacher, Ato thought.

Bello moved on to the biodegradable solar panels on the roofs of the cabins. Ato hadn't even noticed them.

"Richie, will these panels break down to natural particles?" Bello asked.

"Excellent-O, Bello! We think about everything on Nnoma." Richie smiled.

Dzifa gave a "V for Victory" sign. "Profess-O Bello!"

Dzifa sounded so adoring. It grated on Ato's nerves. All she needed now was a cheerleader's skirt and shiny pom-poms, he thought sulkily.

Hafsat eventually emerged from her cabin and made her way down the rungs one cautious step at a time. She was the last one down. Ato felt slightly sorry for her, and as Flock Eleven followed their Guardians along the twisted path that led out of the woods, he hung behind the group to walk with her. Dzifa had skipped off with Bello and hadn't even looked back for him. Bright sunlight hit his face as they emerged from the trees and he lowered his cap to shield his eyes. The route took them past a shallow stream that trickled down to the lake, gurgling sparkling water over the pebbles on its bed. How much fun it would be to sit in it and feel the water cool his skin, he thought.

"My father would have loved to see me here," Ato said.

"So would mine." Hafsat's voice was almost too low to hear.

Ato caught a shadow cross her face. She sounded almost sad when she mentioned her father, but he didn't want to pry. "Are you okay?" he asked.

She nodded. "It just feels strange to be around so many other kids."

"Really?" Ato asked. "There are usually more kids in school."

She shrugged. "I'm homeschooled."

"Oh," he said, surprised. Everyone he knew went to regular school. He wanted to ask her what it was like to be homeschooled, but they had now arrived on an open hillside where Flock Eleven had gathered. Behind them, the calm lake mirrored the blue sky and marshmallow-white puffs of cloud. He led Hafsat through the kids to join Dzifa, Leslie, and, to his annoyance, Bello.

Eyra stood on a boulder waiting for everyone to settle. The breeze teased the ruffles of her long skirt about her ankles.

"How did you like your cabins, Flock Eleven?" she asked, when everyone had sat on the grass. A chorus of delighted answers rose and she nodded her pleasure, smiling.

Eyra gathered her frilly skirt about her, sat on the rock, and crossed her ankles. The sixteen Guardians stood attentively in a semicircle around Flock Eleven.

"Let me tell you about me," she said. Her eyes lit up dreamily. "Nnoma has always been part of my life. When I was a child, every school holiday my father and I would come here to our cabin high up the hill . . ."

Ato listened in rapt attention as Eyra drew a picture of her childhood memories—of holidays spent on the wild island in the woods and forests, with hundreds of bird species and other creatures.

It sounded like Turo, only a million times bigger and with way more birds and animals, Ato thought. Turo was the nature spot near his home that he, Leslie, and Dzifa claimed as their own. It had trees, wild grasses, frogs, lizards, and a deep pond with tall weeds and water lilies.

Eyra's eyes clouded over. "But when I was eighteen, my father died. Nnoma became mine. That's when I began to look around. I noticed that in lands around the lake not far from here, every year fewer and fewer birds remained. And things were changing." She turned to Kai. Her voice was sad. "Kai, will you tell Flock Eleven what has changed?"

Kai's face tightened. "Many of us Guardians were born on lands not far from this lake. Richie, Koku, Frank, and others. But we have lost our villages." A bitter look crossed her face. "We lost them to people who tore up the ground for gold and diamonds. Poisoned the waters with chemicals. Stripped our forests for timber." She looked back across the lake. A look of pain shadowed her face. "The forest was our home. Now it's gone and there are scars left in the ground. Huge muddy pits filled with poisoned water where our forest used to be.

"There's no clean water for my people. Once we could see fish swimming on the riverbed. Now that river is a mud bath. Nothing can live in it." She brushed a hand hard across her glistening eyes. Richie and Eyra both put their arms across Kai's shoulders as Flock Eleven sat in silent dismay. Ato exchanged glances with Leslie and Dzifa. The people who had done that sounded just like the Prophet!

"That's so selfish," Ato burst out.

"And dumb," Dzifa added. "'Cos we can't live on earth if we don't look after it."

"That's when my dream for Nnoma was born," Eyra said gently. "A paradise where the land, air, water, plants, animals, and people were all safe and protected. Where Asafo can grow, and go out to the world, speaking *truth to power*. Young people who are brave and honest enough to tell powerful people when our earth is being treated cruelly and unfairly. Young people who will stand up for what is right even when others try to stop them. Who will not let anyone stand in their way." She stood up. "And this is why we select Asafo—it's a job for brave children."

Beside him, Ato noticed Dzifa and Bello looked at each other approvingly. He scowled. Dzifa had only just met Bello and she was acting like he was her best friend. He wasn't. He was an annoying know-it-all.

Eyra gestured to them to stand up. "Flock Eleven, we're going to take a short walk around Nnoma. After that we'll go to the Flocking Valley. Over there we have something important to do: You're going to form sixteen teams, four children in each team. Each team will take part in eight missions. And after seven days, we'll select the top three teams. They will be our eleventh set of Asafo."

A ripple ran through the gathered children, and they turned to each other.

Dzifa turned to Bello. He raised his furry caterpillar brows. Then she turned to Ato and Leslie. Her lips parted.

Move! Ato thought. Falcon speed.

He turned to Hafsat.

"Hafsat," he said clearly and firmly. "Would you like to join our team? Me, Leslie, and Dzifa?"

CHAPTER SIX

"I CAN'T BELIEVE YOU CHOSE HAFSAT!" DZIFA FUMED, tramping beside Ato along the muddy, gravelly lakeshore. It was alive with wild ducks and more waterbirds than he could count.

They were following Eyra and the Guardians on the walk around Nnoma. Bello was several paces ahead.

She stamped her foot. "I'd already thought about someone for our team!"

Ato glanced behind them. Hafsat's attention had been caught by water weeds with yellow flowers growing along the banks. She was too far off to hear.

"Yeah," he said. "Wonderf-O Profess-O Know-It-All-O Bello."

"At least everything he knows is right."

"So, it would have been okay for you to choose our teammate? But not me?"

"If you didn't want Bello, we could have chosen someone together. Isn't that right, Leslie?"

"Hafsat, Bello, what does it matter?" Leslie said, violently swatting at a beetle buzzing about his ear.

"Bello only cares about himself. I don't even think he would have helped us find the plan, Dzifa," Ato said. He increased the length of his strides, trying not to step on crabs or tiny turtles.

Dzifa pursed her lips so sharply that they looked like a bird's beak. "So you were just being selfish, then, Ato. Thinking about the plan. Well, I can be selfish too. I'll join *Bello's* team."

Leslie's hands dropped to his side, the beetle forgotten. "What?" he exclaimed so loudly that a number of children looked at him.

Dismayed, Ato grabbed her hand. "Dzifa, we're a team."

She snatched her hand away and marched behind the rest of Flock Eleven. "You should have thought about that before you chose Hafsat. You heard Eyra! Asafo aren't just ordinary kids. They're *exceptional*! And then you choose Miss One-Inch-a-Day as a teammate."

She glared at him and hurried over to join Bello.

"You've got to get her back. It's a no-brainer," Leslie urged quietly. They had stopped by a grove, and Eyra had begun talking about cures for diseases that came from trees and plants.

"Is there a problem?" asked a quiet voice. Ato and Leslie whipped their heads around. Hafsat stood behind them, a questioning look in her eyes.

"No," Ato said hurriedly.

"Yes," Leslie admitted.

Ato stepped on Leslie's foot.

"Ouch!" he mumbled.

Hafsat bit her lip. "Is it because you picked me for your team?"

"No . . ."

"Yes," Leslie said.

"Oh." Hafsat's shoulders sagged.

Ato looked furiously at Leslie. Leslie just shrugged.

"Everything will be okay," Ato assured Hafsat.

"Will it rea—" Leslie began. He shut up when Ato glared at him.

Bello had begun telling Eyra about plant medicines that could cure blindness. "Those plants are a vanishing species now," he said, looking around sternly, as though the person responsible for the disappearing plants stood among them.

Dzifa shot Ato a *you see?* look.

"Plant medicines can heal sprained ankles. And snakebites. And toothache," Hafsat added. Her soft voice had a ring of authority. Ato turned in surprise. She went on to list a string of healing herbs . . . cloves and bitterleaf and aidan.

Ato gave Dzifa a *you see?* look back.

He had an example too, he thought. "My grandmother can heal fevers!" he told Eyra. She nodded as he recounted his story. Nana had boiled up neem leaves in a giant bowl and bent him over the steaming bowl with a towel draped over his head, so he could breathe in the bitter healing vapor. "I fell asleep, and in the morning I was better!" he said proudly.

"The world needs more people like your grandmother!" Eyra declared firmly, turning to lead them onward. A wooden signpost announced that they were headed to Rockside, east of the woods and south of the imposing Dawn Locus. Birds wheeled in the air above them, piercing the air with caws and cries.

Rockside was a sweltering expanse of prickly shrubs and giant spiky aloes growing in a valley that stretched all the way down to the lake. Ten-foot boulders jutted from among the thorny plants, like stone huts. Despite their size, they were dwarfed by the shadow of Nnoma's mountain. Rockside was alive not only with birds, but with bugs and beetles and crawling creatures. As they picked their way across the formidable terrain, lizards and small rodents skittered across their paths, raising squeals from startled children.

A tall tree dominated the landscape. From its upper branches, a group of scruffy brown birds with red faces peered down.

"Nasty birds. Aren't those vultures?" Leslie asked.

Ato nodded. "Without them, there'd be a lot more smelly dead animals lying around."

"I read that some kinds even eat animals when they're not yet dead," Leslie said.

"You're right." Bello chipped. "Some of these fellas will do a little dance around a weak creature. A sick one. Or a dying one. Even a helpless newborn. They'll take a light peck there, a nibble there. Then they go for the eyes. Then the tongue, then the flesh. Every last shred of flesh."

"*Ewww.*" Leslie looked like he was going to gag.

On the rest of the walk, Ato noticed that kids had begun forming their teams. He stuck close to Dzifa, whose attitude remained as stony as the landscape they tramped across. To thwart him, Bello kept his arm around Dzifa's shoulder, making jokey comments. Several times she laughed aloud. Ato ground his teeth. Bello's jokes weren't even funny. He was sure Dzifa was laughing to spite him.

Suddenly in his direct line of sight, a boulder momentarily took his attention away from Dzifa. With a stretch of imagination, the boulder looked like a giant wardrobe. It stood probably twelve feet high. Horizontal crags scoured its face like tribal marks, and trailing creepers partially concealed its surface. The crags looked deep, deep enough to be a hiding place. If his father's plan wasn't right at the top, at the Dawn Locus, then this would be his next guess for where it could be.

Where the falcons watch over the valley.

This was where he had to look, Ato thought with rising interest. As soon as possible.

He turned back to Eyra, who was pointing up the mountain. "One of our missions is to climb this," she said. "This mountain is a signal to the world that we on Nnoma will always do what's best for the earth."

"Why is it a signal?" a plump, bespectacled girl asked.

"Because the Dawn Locus stands for the highest form of ourselves," Eyra replied gently. "The people we grow into when we think of the earth and of others, just as much as we think of ourselves—Asafo."

And the plan was up there. Or down here, Ato mused. "I can't wait to climb it and see what it's like up there!" he said aloud.

Richie gave him a cautionary glance. "Let's be clear, Ato, there will be no exploration at the top." He spoke in a no-nonsense tone.

"Sure, we'll have a picnic there to celebrate your climb, but there are steep drops, dangerous crags, and wild falcons. That means being careful."

I'll be back here soon, Ato thought rebelliously. The Guardians planned to keep them herded together like sheep in a flock, but a secret plan was forming in his head. He would soon make his move, soon and swiftly—like a falcon.

After an hour, Eyra led them past a large airy-looking room set on top of a hill. All around the room, wide windows overlooked the hillside and the lake. Inside, the floor was made up of bright red tiles, and comfy-looking couches with colorful floor cushions were set around the room. Above its open double doors hung a wooden sign that read CHIRP AND CHATTER. Ato was sure he would enjoy spending time in there.

Eyra then led them down to a gentle valley bathed in warm sunshine and set between two green hillocks. FLOCKING VALLEY, a sign announced. Three rows of flat gray stone seats were arranged in semicircles and set on the sloping sides of one hillock. Ato reckoned there were about eighty seats in all. Each bore the chiseled image of a bird, etched into the stone in intricate detail: An owl in flight; a gull plunging down into water; a hummingbird hovering over a flower; a woodpecker drilling a tree trunk; an eagle perched on a rock. On each seat there was a different bird. Ato was fascinated. He wondered whether there was a falcon seat, but before he could find out, the places were taken up. He settled on a stork seat close to Dzifa and tried again to get her to join his team. She ignored his efforts and continued chatting with Bello.

A gray stone platform was built into the hillock that rose across from the stone seats. It was wide and flat, and stood about four feet high. Carved into its granite face were the words FLOCK ROCK. Eyra swept up the three steps that led to the top. Kai and Richie joined her, while the other Guardians sat interspersed among Flock Eleven.

Eyra gestured for silence. "Flock Eleven," she said, holding them captive with her gaze. "You will now have fifteen minutes to finally decide who to team up with. Remember, four to a team. After that you get to pick your team names."

Ato grabbed Dzifa's hand. Leslie pushed past Bello and took her other hand in his. Hafsat sat behind them, biting her nails.

Bello gave a superior smile. "Dzifa is joining me and two other boys. You should find someone before all the good people are taken up."

Dzifa gave Ato one final accusing look and began to turn away. But Ato wasn't going to give up. He squeezed her hand.

"Please, Dzifa. I'll . . . I'll . . ." He flashed Hafsat a desperate look. She looked crestfallen.

Dzifa glanced at Hafsat and hesitated.

"I'll leave," Hafsat said quietly.

"Sorry, guys," Bello said lightly. He took Dzifa's hand from Leslie's.

"Sorry, Bello," she muttered, pulling her hand back. She shot Ato a sideways look. "C'mon. Let's go pick out our name."

Ato was weak with relief. Dzifa was back on his team!

CHAPTER SEVEN

ATO SLUMPED BACK IN HIS SEAT. ONE TEAM HAD JUST PICKED the name Excellent Eagles from a hat that Kai held out.

Another had picked Dynamic Doves. Dzifa had just picked their team name.

"Sixteen team names in the hat and we ended up with *Gallant Geese?*" Ato muttered.

"Be grateful I'm with the Gallant Geese," she replied shortly.

Beside them, Bello whooped and raised a "V for Victory" sign. "Fantastic Falcons!" he exclaimed. "I got an awesome team name!" He smirked, looking at Ato. "And just like falcons, we're going to hit our target: become Asafo! Aren't we, guys?" He stretched his arms across the shoulders of the three other members of his team. The girl who had replaced Dzifa clenched her fists and pounded them together.

Ato gritted his teeth and swallowed his envy.

"Coolio, Bello," he managed to say with a smile that was so forced his face ached.

"You got a good name too, fellow competitor," Bello said.

"Gallant Geese. Geese are . . . useful. They . . . eat grass, and . . ." He shrugged. "And they taste good."

Hafsat did not seem to mind what name they got; she was stroking the petals of a purple wildflower. Ato took comfort in the fact that the Brilliant Buzzards were just as unhappy with their name. The Talented Turkeys were squabbling with the Perky Parrots. The Jolly Jays were anything but that: In a squabble over their seats, one of them had trapped his fingers in a wedge underneath the stone slab. It had taken two Guardians and a couple of tense minutes to shift the slab and free his hand.

The teams had also drawn for their mealtimes with Eyra; the Gallant Geese had drawn for dinner on Friday. That cheered Ato up a lot. Friday was only two days away!

Everyone quieted down as Kai read out the rules.

"Flock Eleven, there are eight missions. Complete each one successfully and on time, and your team could earn a full twenty-five points. That's two hundred points. These are the rules:

"One: Stick together. Take part in your team activity. Do not leave your team and go it alone or your team loses points.

"Two: Get along with everyone. Within your team. Outside your team. Don't fight or you lose points.

"Three: Know where your teammates are. Be each other's Guardians. Life means caring about others.

"Four: Follow your Guardian's instructions. The fastest way to drop points is to disobey a Guardian. We're here to protect you. You must cooperate with us."

Ato listened. He was going to have to be careful if he planned to sneak off to look for the plan.

Richie took a step forward. "Flock Eleven, now let me tell you how to win bonus points." He raised one finger. "Helping another team. Helping is a different kind of special. You get loads of points here—up to fifty! We call them Protector Points. They're a big deal. So find ways to earn them and your team could be in the top three with the most points. Those three teams will earn the Asafo badge, and take the pledge to become Protectors of the Earth!

◆ ◆ ◆ ◆ ◆ ◆ ◆

After lunch in the Pecking Bowl, Ato and his teammates headed back Cabinside. Eyra had gone off to have dinner in her cabin with the Super Swifts: each team would have one private meal with her—breakfast, lunch, or dinner.

Dzifa and Hafsat were on amicable terms and followed Ato to have a peek in their cabin before Nest Rest at two p.m. Their first mission was going to be for an hour after dinner: Meet Our Night Neighbors. The Gallant Geese had been assigned Woodside.

Mission One: Asafo understand that there is a place for creatures of the day and of the night. They know their earthly neighbors, and they respect their space, Dzifa read from the note Kai had handed them in the Pecking Bowl.

Ato settled down on the cabin floor and stared at the gleaming black camera in his hand with admiration. Each member of Flock

Eleven had received one along with a flashlight during their lunch hour. "These are *so* cool," he breathed.

"A mission in the dark," Leslie complained, eyeing his new camera with considerably less enthusiasm than Ato. "With snakes and wild animals?"

"It could be fun," Hafsat said slowly. "It sounds simple enough—photograph twenty different night creatures in ninety minutes. Good-quality shots. But the bit about making sure we don't get caught on camera by another team . . . that makes it harder."

"So it's simple—we don't get caught," Dzifa said. "We don't want to drop any points."

"Well . . ." A sly smile had spread across Leslie's face.

Ato looked at him with suspicion. "What have you done?"

Leslie glanced around and whispered something.

Ato drew back. "You *what*? You made a pact with some of the other teams?"

"Yeah." Leslie grinned. "The Wonderful Warblers, Brilliant Buzzards, and the Fantastic Falcons. They're all Woodside, with us. It's simple. We don't take pictures of them. They don't take pictures of us. Win-win, right?"

"Yes, but . . ." Ato bit his thumbnail doubtfully. "It sounds a little like cheating."

"Well, I didn't want to be hiding from wild animals *and* from other kids. That's way too much for one night," Leslie explained remorselessly.

"Anyway, pact or no pact, we're going to be looking at all the night pictures at the Chirp and Chatter tomorrow morning, so do not get caught on anyone else's camera," Dzifa said. "Now let's check out our cameras."

The next half hour flew by as Ato and his teammates fiddled happily with their cameras. They closed the cabin shutters to take pictures in the dark and tried out the heat sensor function. Ato set a bucket of water on the table to test out the underwater function. This did not go well. The bucket tipped over, dumping its contents onto Leslie, who was on the floor taking a moving picture of a ladybird on the doorpost.

"You dropped something," Hafsat said, as Leslie grumpily emptied his soggy pockets. She reached down and picked up a small can about twice the size of her thumb.

"Pepper spray?" she read in surprise.

"Gimme that." Leslie snatched it from her.

Just as quickly, Ato whipped the wooden can from Leslie's hand. "All-natural," he remarked, inspecting the label. "No wonder you got it past the bee checkpoint!" He handed it back to his friend.

"You never saw it," Leslie muttered. He pushed it deep into his wet pocket. "I had to protect myself."

Dzifa shook her head. "Leslie, this is useless on birds. They don't feel heat from peppers. Not the way other animals do."

"Well, it's not just birds I was thinking about. What about other wild animals?"

"What are you expecting? Lions? Hyenas?" she snorted.

"I dunno. I just need to make sure I leave this place alive."

Tinkling chimes from outside signaled the start of Nest Rest: Hafsat and Dzifa went back to their cabins and silence fell on Nnoma.

◆ ◆ ◆ ◆ ◆ ◆ ◆

Five hours later, Ato crouched stock-still below a tree in the thick darkness of Woodside. The air was thick with the smells of rich earth, wood perfume, rotting vegetation, animal scents, and the sweet aroma of forest fruits and flowers. Mission One had begun.

Four teams had been assigned to this wooded part of the island. The other teams were on Lakeside, Rockside, and Hillside. The night-vision goggles that he had been provided fit snugly and gave everything around him an eerie green glow. He felt like a spy.

His teammates huddled beside him in the dark. Their Guardian for the night, the heavyset Koku, led the way. How alive the dark was when daytime hunters and creatures had gone to bed, Ato thought. The high-pitched *kwreeek kwreeek kwreeeek* of katydids and crickets dominated the cooing, whistling, screeching, slithering, scurrying, and fluttering of other night creatures.

"The daytime competition has gone to bed. Now the masters of the night are out," Koku whispered.

Dzifa was already snapping pictures of the large green and brown crickets.

Hafsat had noticed a strange green glow scattered in patches about the ground.

"Luminous fungi," Koku explained. "That light draws insects. The insects then spread fungal spores everywhere so the mushrooms can grow in other places."

The glowing mushrooms were too much of a draw for Hafsat. "Pretty," she breathed, photographing them. Dzifa had to tug her arm to pull her away.

"Animals, animals, not plants, Hafsat!" she clucked.

Suddenly a sharp *whrock whrock whrock* cut the night air.

Koku gestured to them to stand still. In the dark ahead of them, a speckled bird with long wings scuttled along the ground.

"A nightjar," Ato whispered, recognizing it. He clicked his shutter swiftly. "It can sound like a dog, I remember!"

They crept on in the darkness. Ato was all too aware of the rustling of other teams above the sounds of the night.

WHOOOSH! A rush of air swept over Ato's head and a large dark form swooped low above them. He fell to the ground in fright. Koku helped him up, pointing to a large owl that had settled on the branch of a tree across from them. Its intelligent saucer eyes beheld them quizzically.

"They can fly soundlessly," Koku said as Ato and his friends recovered their composure enough to take pictures of the bird of prey. "And he can see us better than we can see him. Pity the poor mouse that chooses to come this way."

A few feet later, Hafsat began taking pictures of purple night-blooming flowers that had attracted large moths to their petals.

"Take pictures of the moths, not the flowers," Dzifa reminded her in a sharp tone.

Hafsat sighed and followed them as they edged through the woods, twigs snapping underfoot on the damp leaf-strewn ground. Along the way, they took pictures of rodents with glittering eyes, tree mammals, and several kinds of toads. Then Ato paused and turned curiously to Koku. A raucous squabbling and cackling had begun in a tree above them.

"Flying foxes," Koku said. "Bats. Fighting for wild fruit. This is a feeding tree." Ato trained his camera on the bustling creatures.

Splat!

Leslie gave a muffled squeal.

"Eww——it's warm," he said, disgusted.

Koku chuckled in the dark. "Yes, they do that. Spit out chaff from the fruit. And often it's not just spit."

Leslie's groan of revulsion halted abruptly as a hairy, four-legged creature shuffled into a clearing a few feet ahead of them. Ato stared at it, feeling his palms begin to sweat. It was thick-bodied and as high as his waist, with hooves, a long snout, and short tusks protruding from its lower jaw.

"A wild boar," Koku whispered. "These are the biggest animals on the island. Just stay still. Many of these nighttime creatures just want to be left alone."

Ato and his team got in several good shots before the bush pig ambled off, grunting and snuffling at the ground with its snout.

Something small, dark, and very fast hurtled across Ato's feet. Hafsat squeaked and jumped.

"Just another bush rat," Koku said soothingly. "Excellent for soups."

Leslie gave a stifled groan.

Then Ato froze.

A creature that looked part fox, part cat, and part raccoon stood ahead of them, with powerful-looking hind legs. It had black spots and stripes on a silver-gray coat, and a menacing black band across its eyes.

"It's a civet," Koku said.

Dzifa and Ato clicked together, simultaneously capturing it before it slunk off into the undergrowth.

A plaintive wailing sound drifted toward them on the night air.

"Can you hear that?" Dzifa murmured.

Ato frowned, unable to believe his ears. "Is that a . . . a *baby* crying?"

Koku nodded and put a finger to his lips. "Bush baby," he whispered. "I think it's over there." Dzifa, Leslie, and Hafsat took tentative steps in the direction where he was pointing.

At that moment, from the corner of his eye Ato saw a shadow move. He whipped his head around. It was an aardvark! The dull brown animal had ears like a hare, a hump like a camel, hoof-like claws at the end of its feet, a long snout, and a thick tail.

Quivering with excitement, he raised his camera. Just as he was about to click, he was startled by a shriek behind him. He whirled around. A tall figure stood, camera raised. There was a click. Ato gasped. When he turned back to see the aardvark, the creature had vanished into the bush.

"Are you crazy? What was that for?" Ato spluttered,

recognizing Bello through his goggles. "Now it's gone!" A thought flashed. "Wait, did you get *me* in your picture?"

Just then, familiar tinkly chimes echoed through the woods.

"Mission One is over," Koku announced.

CHAPTER EIGHT

ATO WAS STILL MAD AT BREAKFAST THE NEXT MORNING.

"What a snake!" he fumed to his teammates. He took a savage bite into a fonio roll. "Bello did that on purpose! Took a picture of the aardvark, and then he scared it off! And then he took a picture of me. So much for your stupid pact," he said, turning on Leslie.

"Maybe he'll delete the picture," Leslie said, not sounding like he believed his own words.

Ato hadn't been able to say a word to Bello last night—the Guardians had been all over the place making sure Flock Eleven got back safely to their cabins.

This morning Bello stuck close to one of the Guardians, leaving Ato no room to confront him. Breakfast itself was a lively affair. Eyra had come in and sung a zany tune with them. The Jolly Jays had gone to enjoy their breakfast in her garden, bickering on the way out about who got to hold Eyra's hands.

An hour later Flock Eleven was back at the Chirp and Chatter to view pictures from Mission One. The Jolly Jays were back from their breakfast, arguing about which one of them Eyra had spent the most time talking to.

The TV display started, showing vivid pictures taken by other teams during Mission One. Each group shared something about an animal they had spotted.

The Excellent Eagles had taken more than twenty sharp pictures from Mission One, including a prize picture of a python coiled up in thick loops around a branch.

"Pythons like birds. And eggs. And rats and mice. But not people," one of the Eagles explained. There was an audible sigh of relief from Flock Eleven.

The Talented Turkeys had also photographed more than twenty animals, including a pangolin! Ato gawked at its picture on the screen. It had curled up into a protective ball, front legs covering its head. Its large overlapping scales looked like a suit of armor. One of the Turkeys, a girl with a squeaky voice, rattled at top speed about pangolins vanishing because people killed them for food, used their scales in traditional medicines, and chopped down the trees in which they lived.

Several teams had taken decent wildlife pictures, though there were a good number of fuzzy images that looked nothing like the animals they were supposed to be.

"Those could be anything from a pile of rags to an old shoe," Dzifa muttered to Ato, looking critically at the Perky Parrots' picture of a tortoise.

Groans and titters alike rose as several kids saw themselves caught on camera by other teams. Ato gritted his teeth and looked over at Bello.

The Super Swifts were caught on camera asleep between two giant tree roots. They had been watching out for a bush baby, they explained sheepishly.

The Jolly Jays had misplaced two cameras and began an argument about who'd had them last.

Finally, Dzifa spoke for the Gallant Geese; they had twenty-seven pictures, several more than were required. Most kids had never heard of a civet.

"Does it bite?" a scared-looking Splendid Sandpiper asked.

"Yes, if you're an egg, a fruit, a mouse, or an insect," Dzifa quipped, grinning. "This guy doesn't turn his nose up at much. He'll even eat a dead animal. He sleeps in the bush and in trees during the day and wakes up at night."

Next were the Fantastic Falcons. Ato scowled when his surprised face flashed on the screen. Bello spoke smoothly about the aardvark he had caught on camera, and jealousy surged within Ato. If Bello hadn't scared it away, they would have had a picture of the aardvark too!

Eventually, every group had made their presentation, and the top three score table lit up the screen:

SCORES

TEAM	MISSION ONE: Points out of 25	POSITION OUT OF 16
Talented Turkeys	24	1st
Dynamic Doves	22	2nd
Fantastic Falcons	22	2nd

Underneath the top three table was a list. The Gallant Geese were in fourth place with twenty-one, with the Excellent Eagles in fifth. At the bottom of the table, with six points, were the Brilliant Buzzards and the Super Swifts. The Buzzards hugged each other, overjoyed at having scored some points, while the Super Swifts slumped in mute misery. Ato forced a smile. Fourth place! The Gallant Geese could have been in the top three, if Bello hadn't played that dirty trick.

CHAPTER NINE

"WELL DONE, GEESE," BELLO SAID TO ATO SHORTLY afterward. They had left the Chirp and Chatter and Mission Two had begun: the Canopy Walk. It had started with a steep climb up several sets of wooden rungs that led to a circular platform built around a 120-foot-high pole.

"It's just a competition," Bello continued. "Don't take it personally."

Ato resisted the urge to say something rude. He needed all his attention for Mission Two. The task was to photograph at least thirty birds within ninety minutes—while crossing a swinging walkway suspended one hundred and twenty feet above the ground.

It would have been easy enough to walk the planks, Ato reckoned, if it wasn't for the birds and nests made from bamboo that had been hooked onto the rope rail of the walkway. They were feather-light, and if the walkway rocked too violently, a bird or a nest would fall off. For every one that dropped from the walkway, a point was dropped. Each team had been given a printed note signed by Eyra's hand. It was titled *Mission Two Principle*:

Humans often disturb the natural world. In Mission Two the Asafo understands that we share this globe with other creatures. The Asafo respects them and respects their right to be. The Asafo protects the earth and does not disturb the environment.

Once on the first circular platform, Ato took a deep breath. A wooden plank stretched out from the platform like a narrow bridge. On either side of it, thick rope netting rose above head-height to keep walkers from plunging to the distant ground. This wooden bridge led to a second wooden platform built around another tall pole. From that platform, a second bridge led to a third platform. On and on they went, from bridge to platform. Ato counted twelve sections in all.

The walk was not for the faint-hearted. One Super Swift, a girl with wide earnest eyes, swiftly fainted on the high wooden platform. A Buzzard, a boy nearly six feet tall with a fuzzy beard, clutched the center pole with his eyes screwed shut, shouting, "Mama, Mama, I don't want to die!" It had taken three Guardians to pry his arms from around the pole. A Magnificent Macaw who had previously thrilled everyone with her backflips took one look at the drop over the side of the platform and propelled a magnificent amount of her breakfast onto the foliage below.

The Jolly Jays followed. They were braver than most other teams. One of them tried to take a shot of a rare gray parrot, overbalanced, and accidentally tripped his teammate. This triggered first an argument, then a shoving competition on the bridge. Bamboo birds and nests rained down like confetti onto the treetops beneath them. Two Guardians ushered them away to cool off on the next platform.

The Gallant Geese were next. Ato took another deep breath. Hafsat was breathing in fast shallow gasps beside him.

"I don't like heights," she whispered.

"We're Geese—we can fly high," he assured her, trying to sound brave. From the look on her face, he expected her to throw up like the unfortunate Macaw.

Ato swallowed. He heard Eyra's words at breakfast about Mission Two. *"In Mission Two the Asafo understands that time is not always on our side. That whole species have been wiped out because we moved too late to help. The Asafo moves quickly. The Asafo looks around carefully. The Asafo notices everything that shares this earth with us."*

The treetops stretched out like a green sea beneath him. The first plank swayed when he stepped on it and he steadied himself on the ropes. It rocked more violently. His heart sank as a bamboo bird fluttered to the ground. Sweat trickled down his temple. Behind him, Dzifa groaned. He steadied himself and began to inch across the plank.

"It's so . . . shaky." Hafsat's voice quavered. "What if one of the boards cracks? What if the rope snaps?"

"We don't have time to think about stuff like that, Hafsat," Dzifa said, treading after her with cat-like steps.

By the second platform Ato had gotten the hang of the plank walk and he began to take in the glorious three-sixty view of the treetops. A large bird with gleaming blue feathers and a dark crest atop its head fluttered onto a nearby branch, close enough to touch. A great blue turaco! He'd seen one at a bird reserve Nana had taken him to. He captured a picture of it.

Leslie crept toward the second platform, looking doubtfully at the ropes. "It *has* been five years since any other kids came here. Has anyone been checking this wood-and-rope thing? What if it's rotting?" He gave the walkway all his attention, testing each plank with his feet as if he expected it to give way beneath his weight. The colorful birds and spectacular treetop view got none of his attention. He made it to the end of the first bridge without dislodging a single bamboo bird or nest, and without taking a single picture.

Ato was lost in the wonder of the canopy walkway. His teammates, the other teams, the Guardians, the heat of the day—everything faded away, and he was a falcon again. His super-sharp eyesight caught dozens of birds around him: a yellow-bearded greenbul twittering from a slender branch, a wattle-eye with bright red cheeks, a long-tailed hawk, a cuckooshrike with stunning blue feathers, a serpent eagle perched on the highest branches of a tree. He could outfly any of these birds.

Ninety minutes went faster than he wanted them to. He was eventually back on the leafy ground beside Leslie and Dzifa, looking up as Richie and Kai guided Hafsat inch by painful inch along a bridge.

"It's nice she's at least moving," he said to a glum-looking Dzifa as bamboo birds and nests fluttered down, disturbed by Hafsat's wobbly passage. He hadn't thought Hafsat would have been such a scaredy cat. He felt bad for his team, but he felt sorry for Hafsat too.

Dzifa gave him a sour look. "Ato, *nice* is not enough here. There's nothing gallant about not being able to walk across a few wooden boards."

"And there's nothing hygienic about drinking from other people's bottles." Leslie grimaced, watching as Kai took a long drink from Richie's water flask.

Hafsat eventually completed the canopy walk. "That was something else," she said with a sigh, sinking down onto the exposed roots of a large tree. She had soon recovered enough to take pictures of coned flowers growing between the tree roots.

A short while later, Flock Eleven had gathered in the Chirp and Chatter, and after all photographs had been shared, the top three score table flashed up on the screen.

TEAM	MISSION TWO: Points out of 50	POSITION OUT OF 16
Dynamic Doves	47	1st
Talented Turkeys	46	2nd
Fantastic Falcons	46	2nd

The Gallant Geese had dropped to sixth place on the list beneath the table. Dzifa slid a dissatisfied look in Hafsat's direction.

Bello strolled past with his team on the way out of the Chirp and Chatter. "There was always only going to be space for three at the top," he said unnecessarily loudly to his team.

"I'm sorry about being so slow," Hafsat said to Ato as Flock Eleven settled on the hillside to enjoy the lake breeze before lunch.

"It's okay," he said weakly, squinting over his right shoulder at the Dawn Locus. Falcons circled the peak, like dark shadows high against the blue sky. He hadn't had a moment to look for the plan. And the rule about teams staying together made looking for it even harder. A fist of doubt squeezed his heart. It was going to be a big job.

Hafsat must have thought he was admiring the view. "Isn't it gorgeous here?" she asked.

He breathed out slowly. "My dad helped to make this island a place that children could visit."

She sat up. "Really?"

"He's dead."

She sighed. "I know what that feels like."

"Yours too, huh?" Ato asked in understanding. He reached over and squeezed her hand.

She sighed and said, "Tell me about your dad."

And Ato told her what he could about the father he'd never known—the strong, good, and caring person everyone said he was. How he'd helped to carve out the most difficult part of the path leading up to the Dawn Locus, before the first Asafo arrived. How he'd died suddenly on Nana's old orange sofa. And the letter he had written to his baby son while he was working on Nnoma.

"That's sad," she murmured, when he'd finished. A few moments later, she spoke again, almost apologetically. "Ato . . . this is a big place to be looking for a plan."

"Well, I'm going to start looking," Ato whispered. "Tonight."

"Where?" Hafsat asked.

Ato smiled cagily. He wasn't sure whether she could keep a secret. And in any case, he hadn't even told his best friends. Leslie would definitely try to stop him.

"Tell me about your dad," he said instead.

"The thing about my dad is . . . was . . . umm." She lowered her head and sighed. "I don't like talking about it."

Ato nodded. "We don't have to talk about it," he assured her. But he was still curious. What was "it" that Hafsat didn't want to talk about?

CHAPTER TEN

THAT NIGHT, AFTER DINNER, ATO STUCK HIS HAND OUT OF his cabin door and helped Hafsat up the last rung. He had asked his team to meet for a chat before bedtime chimes.

Dzifa was already cross-legged on the floor rug in the cozy cabin Ato shared with Leslie. Hafsat settled on a cushion beside Leslie, who was peering out the window at the night sky and muttering about rain. Ato fervently hoped he was wrong. He needed a dry night for what he was planning.

Next, Ato drew up four mugs of cinnamon-spiced cocoa from the pulley-operated tree tray that the cooks set out after dinner. He handed the steaming mugs around and then sat down next to Dzifa. The rich fragrance of the bedtime beverage mingled with the sweet wood smell of the cabin.

"So what did you want us here for?" Dzifa demanded.

He licked his lips uncomfortably. "I need to apologize to you, Dzifa. I asked Hafsat to join us without asking you first. So, I just wanted you to know I'm sorry."

"Accepted. It would just have been nice to have been asked."

Hafsat apologized for her slowness on the walkway. "It was scary," she said plaintively. "I don't know what else I can do."

"Be better, that's what you can do," Dzifa said shortly.

Ato cut in hastily. "From now, let's be the best team. Let's become Asafo. And let's find my dad's plan."

Dzifa set her mug down. "Let's do the math too. We're sixth—not good. Tomorrow we have three missions. That's one hundred and fifty points. Let's get them *all*." She gave Hafsat a level look.

"I agree," Ato said, extending his fist for a group bump. "So can we promise now to be a great team, get all the points, and find the plan? Please?"

Somewhere in the distance, thunder rumbled. The breeze picked up, and tree branches rustled against the cabin walls. Ato shivered. He wished he had company for later. But going solo was risky enough. A partner would make it more likely that Guardians would spot them.

"It might rain tonight," Leslie said. "Even the birds are quieting down."

Ato discreetly crossed his fingers. Please, God, no rain, he begged silently.

"How do birds know when it's going to rain?" Hafsat asked.

"They listen to the feather forecast," Dzifa shot in. Everyone burst into laughter.

The next twenty minutes were spent like a team of friends, with jokes and laughter. When the bedtime chimes eventually carried into their cabin, Ato was sorry to see Dzifa and Hafsat leave for the night.

◆ ◆ ◆ ◆ ◆ ◆ ◆

An hour later, with Leslie gently snoring, Ato crept down the rungs. After their first mission he'd decided he could brave being out alone on the island in the dark. He had his night-vision goggles and his flashlight, and a thick strong stick.

He stepped cautiously. There had been a light drizzle and the soft earth conspired with him, muffling his footsteps. He steadied his breathing. There was no time during the day, so this was the only way to do it. Fortunately, thick clouds above had hidden the moon and stars, but there would be a few Guardians on watch, he knew, so he'd have to be careful. He scurried through Cabinside, out of Woodside, and began the tedious journey toward Rockside accompanied by the sounds of chirring and screeching night creatures. His own breathing sounded loud and ragged in his ears, echoing the wind, which was whipping up briskly. After a few unpleasant encounters on his shin and forehead with low branches and hidden rocks, he could finally see it in the green glow of his goggles: the wardrobe-shaped boulder in the valley at the foot of the mountain. This was the place where anything could possibly be hidden.

Something shrieked in a tree above him and he nearly yelled in fright. Once his heart rate had returned to normal, he began to feel around the boulder, shining his flashlight on it. He pushed his stick into the crags and fissures on its stone face, as deep as it could go. Sweeping the stick from side to side within each crack, he tried to feel for something, anything. He swept out dust. Rubble.

Old leaves and twigs. Shards of splintered rock. But no plan. He wanted to scream in frustration.

A flash of lightning temporarily blinded him. It was time to go. Throwing away the stick in disgust, he began to trek back. He had only taken a few steps when he froze. Voices. People. They were arguing. Guardians! He ducked behind a spreading aloe and cursed silently. Of all the places on the island they could be at this moment! He steadied his breathing and remained silent, huddled behind the giant plant. How lucky he was that the ground was damp. Dry crackly undergrowth would have given him away.

A voice snapped out in the dark.

"No! Not now. Not ever!"

He knew that voice—Kai's. With a shudder, he pressed back against the aloe. The plant's unforgiving spikes pierced his skin. He steeled himself to suffer in silence.

"But Kai, these are good people! Smart people with smart plans. People who care about us. They know what's best for us. Let's listen to what they have to say!"

"Again, no, Richie! I will not listen to them!"

"But they can help us."

"You fool, you call this help?" she spat. "Then let us die, Richie! Let every one of us die with Nnoma's secret!"

Nnoma's secret! Again! Was this the same one Nana had talked about on the phone? Blood pounded in his temple. What was this secret? And why did Kai want everyone to die because of it?

"You're unbelievable, Kai! Look at how long we've suffered! And then after that, five years—five long years—don't you care about that? Don't you want this to end? All this fear? All this hiding? Don't you want things to be good for our people?"

"No, I don't, Richie."

"Listen to me, Kai—"

"I will not listen, Richie. Not to you. Not to them. Not today. Not tomorrow. Not ever." Kai's voice was menacing. "So shut up about this. Shut up forever, I warn you."

From a corner of his goggles, Ato spotted movement. His mouth went dry.

It was a snake.

Thin, long, and brown. It slithered toward him, making no sound over the rocky ground.

Terrified, he drew back against the aloe. Behind him, the two Guardians raged at each other. Tears sprang in his eyes as the aloe spike pierced through his shirt into his flesh.

Still the snake drew closer, its forked tongue flicking menacingly. The reptile slid on its belly to within a foot of him. With a muffled shriek, he dived across behind another aloe.

Without changing course, the snake slid past.

The voices immediately went silent.

"Is anyone there?" Richie called.

Ato covered his mouth with his hands.

"Did I imagine that?" Richie asked.

"No, someone's out here." Her voice was terse. "Frank?"

Through his goggles, Ato could see them, green figures getting closer.

His heart drummed up a panicked beat. It was all over. He tensed up for the inevitable.

And then mercy dropped from heaven. Literally. Huge heavy raindrops hammered down, thudding against his skin and sending the two Guardians hurrying away from Rockside. Ato remained huddled in position with his face pressed into his knees to protect himself from the pounding rain. After a few minutes, when he was sure they had gone, he ran, half-blinded by the downpour, along the slippery and muddy trail all the way back to his cabin. Scrambling up the rungs, he peeled off his soggy clothes, changed in the dark, and crawled back into his bunk, heart still pounding. How close he had come to crossing Kai!

CHAPTER ELEVEN

THE NEXT MORNING AT THE PECKING BOWL, THE AROMA OF grilled fish, warm sorghum bread, fruit, and spiced porridge wafted over the cool August air. Ato settled at his table and glanced around furtively while he narrated the incident of the night before to his team.

Leslie drummed the table with nervous fingers. "All that time I was sleeping, you were creeping around in the dark? Ato, you could've gotten hurt! Or lost! Or drowned! And by now there'd be a search party looking for you and all that. And for nothing . . . 'cos you didn't find the plan. Plus, it's against the rules, so we could have lost points."

"But he didn't get hurt. And he's not lost. And he did find out something," Dzifa said. She turned to Ato. "There's some secret on this island. You should have asked your nana about it. Or Max."

"Eyra knows about it too," Ato said, keeping his voice low so that Bello and the others at their table wouldn't hear him.

Hafsat crumbled her sorghum bread into bits. "Do you think we could ask her when we meet her for dinner?"

"I dunno," Ato said uncertainly. "Everything I know is from eavesdropping." He felt uncomfortable.

"Well, we should keep an eye on Kai," Leslie muttered. "She wants us to die and she wants us to suffer and she doesn't care that Nnoma was closed for five years. I think she's dangerous."

"Don't let her see you watch her," Ato warned. "She might get suspicious. Do you think she could be one of Nnoma's enemies? The ones my father spoke about in his letter?"

It was impossible to figure out why Kai had threatened Richie.

On the table behind them the Wonderful Warblers, who'd had dinner with Eyra the night before, hadn't stopped warbling about Eyra and her mysterious cook.

"That cook—he's a magician! He's blind, but he moves around the garden as if he can see, not groping about or anything."

"You should see him with a knife! He chops vegetables and flowers like this!" "This" was a dizzying display of slashes with table cutlery, which was swiftly ended by the sharp-eyed Kai just as Eyra sailed into the Pecking Bowl.

A buzz sparked around the room as Eyra called everyone up to do a hop-cross-skip dance, the skirt of her long dress swirling like a cloud. Afterward, she floated out of the Pecking Bowl with the Magnificent Macaws fluttering dizzily behind her for their Friday breakfast.

An hour later the Magnificent Macaws returned, prattling about their sumptuous breakfast underneath a tree, how much fun Eyra had been, and how very, very strange her cook was. Mission Three—Camouflage Hunt—was now ready to begin.

Their mission principle read: *The Asafo see what is unseen and hear what is unheard. With every step that they take, they know they share their space with ten thousand invisible comrades.*

The Gallant Geese, determined to claw back missing points, gave it their all. Ato spotted a scops owl, perched in a narrow fork of the tree, its feathers blending perfectly with the tree bark, making it almost impossible to see.

Hafsat photographed a large "leaf" that, to Dzifa's astonishment, unfurled its wings and skittered away. That was a ghost mantis, Richie told them, adding that it was in the same family as the praying mantis, the one famous for eating its partner's head.

Leslie tumbled backward when a "rock" that Dzifa had trained her eye on sprang arms and legs and hopped away.

"We might as well be in the Amazon." He sighed. "How can toads get so big?"

All the while, during their mission, they kept a close watch on Kai. Once, Ato crept too close to her, trying to listen in on a conversation she was having with a sweet-faced Guardian called Bea. Unfortunately, Kai spotted him. Her baleful glare sent him stumbling away, hot-faced.

Though they discovered nothing useful about Kai, the Gallant Geese photographed a cunningly concealed chameleon, several moths and butterflies, a tortoise, a grass snake, caterpillars, land snails, geckos, and stick insects, all exactly the same color and pattern as their backgrounds.

When the results of Mission Three were released, the Gallant Geese were ecstatic.

TEAM	MISSION THREE: Points out of 75	POSITION OUT OF 16
Talented Turkeys	70	1st
Gallant Geese	68	2nd
Dynamic Doves	66	3rd

The Excellent Eagles were in fourth place, and the Fantastic Falcons had dropped to sixth position because one of them had tried to cheat, taking a picture of a leaf and trying to convince the Guardians that it was an insect.

Things were going very well, the Geese agreed, as they headed up for lunch with the rest of the Flock. If only they knew why Kai wanted everyone to die.

♦ ♦ ♦ ♦ ♦ ♦ ♦

After Nest Rest that day, Flock Eleven stood close to the lake's shore. Rows and rows of long, hollow bamboo stems had been arranged along the grassy bank while three Guardians, Koku, Frank, and Bea, demonstrated how to use the lightweight wood for Mission Four: Raft-Building.

Their Asafo principle for Mission Four read: *The Asafo travels through the earth wisely and resourcefully using what the earth offers, without waste or pollution.*

"Bamboo stems are perfect for floating, because they're filled with air," Koku explained. He helped the other two to form a square frame with four bamboo poles, which they lashed together with thick vines.

"Each team will make a raft," Frank added. "You will then sail it halfway around the island to a cave marked with your team's name. You earn points for building a good raft, and more points for doing it in good time, so don't spend the whole day on the job."

Kai took over. "At the cave, you'll find a set of instructions for your next task, Mission Five. A Guardian will follow each team—for your safety, not to give you advice. Each team must work alone. You cannot talk to another team or get help from them. Otherwise . . ."

"You lose points!" Flock Eleven chorused.

She smiled thinly. "Smart kids."

The Guardians laid several thinner bamboo rods side by side over the square frame, tying these too together. Soon they had a solid-looking raft. They slid it onto the lake, using extra bamboo poles as rollers underneath it. Flock Eleven cheered as the vessel bobbed impressively on the calm water.

"Your time starts now, teams," Kai announced. "You have ninety minutes to build your rafts. And another ninety minutes to return here after Mission Five down at the caves."

The Brilliant Buzzards were first to get a decent-looking raft, which they dragged to the lake. Its rear end promptly sank below the water. Its front end stuck out like the bow of the *Titanic*.

"Guess it's not enough to look like a raft. It should act like a raft," Dzifa panted to her teammates while they secured extra lashings of vine around their frame.

The Magnificent Macaws were ready, confidently shoving their raft onto the lake. It floated! The Macaws clambered onto it. It creaked ominously, then immediately fell apart, its bamboo stems floating out in different directions.

"Ha! I knew they'd finished too fast," Leslie muttered, tugging a stem into place.

"Make sure your bamboo stems are *really* tightly attached together," Richie called out, vainly trying to hide the amused twinkle in his eyes.

Both the Macaws and the Buzzards hauled their ill-fated rafts back to shore and began to fix them.

The Falcons, Doves, Turkeys, and Eagles were making fast progress. "Let's keep moving," Dzifa urged. Beside them, two Sandpipers had taken a break to play sword games with their bamboo stems.

Ato's arm trembled as he worked feverishly with his team to finish their raft. As they secured a heavy corner pole in place, Hafsat let go of it too early. Its full weight landed on her careless hand. Hard.

"Oww," she squealed, hopping about, her face twisted in agony.

Ato could tell Dzifa was suppressing her annoyance. There were now only three of them working on the raft, while Kai got an ice pack for Hafsat's throbbing hand. One of the Guardians, a lady with slim hairy arms, held up the time card. Fifteen minutes to go.

The Fantastic Falcons were ready first, with fourteen minutes to go.

"I'll bet it will sink," Leslie said firmly.

Ato silently hoped so too, but he had to give grudging respect as the Fantastic Falcons raft bobbed commandingly on the water. With their life vests securely strapped on, the Falcons hopped onto their raft, waved in triumph to the others, and paddled away with wooden oars. A Guardian followed in another small raft.

A couple of minutes later, the Talented Turkeys were on the water, floating on a raft that looked sturdy enough to carry a car in addition. The Eagles set off successfully as well. Shortly afterward, with eleven minutes left on the clock, the Gallant Geese were ready.

Their raft was heavier than he expected and Ato had a sinking feel as they slid it over bamboo poles, down the muddy bank, into the water. But it floated!

CHAPTER TWELVE

Dzifa threw her head back and roared, a primal war cry.

"I hope there are no crocodiles in the water," Leslie said, as they paddled away slowly. Richie stroked silently behind them in a small canoe.

Hafsat's strokes were clumsy and out of rhythm and the raft began to rock unsteadily. Dzifa tut-tutted her frustration.

"It's my hand, Dzifa," Hafsat pouted. "It hurts . . . Ooh, look at those!" she squealed, forgetting her pain and pointing at a flock of white birds near the shore. They had black patches on their wings and backs. "What are those?"

Ato recognized them at once. "Avocets! You can always tell by those upturned bills and blue legs."

"Why do they sweep their heads like that from side to side on the water?" Hafsat asked curiously.

"Scything," Ato replied, proud of what he knew. And it was all thanks to Nana, he thought. "They're looking for food—tiny fish, water bugs, and stuff."

"Hafsat," Dzifa barked. "Keep rowing! There's no time for sightseeing!"

Hafsat sulkily began paddling again. They lurched past hordes of birds wading through the shallow water on the banks and mudflats. Ato longed to slow down to admire them, but the clock was ticking. Several hot, sweaty minutes later, they rounded a sharp bend in the bank. Ahead of them was a row of small dark caves several feet up from the shore. Here, there were very few birds, just gravel and rocks.

Leslie shuddered. "I hope we don't have to go into those."

They did. Every cave had a team name painted on a wooden board that was nailed above its opening. Several other teams had made it ashore and crossed the muddy bank to their caves.

The Gallant Geese heaved their raft onto the bank and squelched across the soggy ground to the mouth of their cave. Richie stayed several paces behind them. He sat on a rock and looked into the distance, whistling a tune.

"It's so dark," Leslie groaned, squinting at the narrow opening.

"What do we do, Richie?" Hafsat asked, uncertainty on her face.

"Sorry, I can't break the rules," the Guardian replied from his sunny perch.

"We've just got to go in," Dzifa declared.

"Hey, look at this." Leslie pointed. Right beside them, wedged into the rock by the mouth of the cave, was a little pail with a lid. A note with two simple words had been pasted on the lid: *Cool Off*.

Ato lifted the lid. "Popsicles?"

They looked at each other in puzzlement.

"Cool off, indeed," Dzifa grumbled. "It's to distract us!"

Bello and his team had emerged from their cave. "There's probably nothing in these," he called from where he stood a few yards away. He clambered back onto his raft with his teammates. "It's all a trick. Smartest person is the one who guesses that and beats the clock!"

"Wow, they're done already!" Leslie exclaimed, watching as the Falcons paddled away back in the direction of Hillside. "What d'you think?"

"I don't trust him," Ato said grimly. "Let's get inside."

"But I want a popsicle," Leslie protested, taking the frozen treat.

"Me too. I'm hot," said Hafsat. She reached for one and began sucking on it.

Dzifa rolled her eyes and tugged at Ato's sleeve. "Let's check this cave out."

Ato bent low to enter the narrow opening. It led into a dim tunnel, with moss-covered rock making up the walls on both sides. Inside, the air smelled moist and cool. The tunnel extended a few feet ahead, then bent sharply to the right. After the bright sunshine outside, Ato's eyes struggled to adjust to the dark. He groped about in the dark, feeling the rough stone walls. There appeared to be shadowy rectangular forms along one side of the wall. It was difficult to see exactly what they were.

"They feel like . . . picture frames," Ato said, reaching up to touch the walls.

"What are we—owls? How are we supposed to see them?" Dzifa fretted.

From outside, Ato heard his name. Leslie was calling. It sounded urgent. He and Dzifa stumbled out of the cave, blinking in the bright sunlight.

"Look!" Leslie held out his popsicle: Clearly printed on the slim wooden stick was the word: *UNDER*.

"And look at mine," Hafsat said, holding out her stick. *FLASHLIGHT* was printed on it.

Ato and Dzifa grabbed the other two, chomping off cold chunks of pineapple ice to reveal the words: *THE* and *PAIL*.

"Flashlight under the pail," they yelled together.

In one yank, Ato had dislodged the pail, and picked up a slim flashlight tucked into the hollow of the rock. Back in the cave, its yellow glare lit up the walls. Two rows of pictures were now in bright view on the rocky stone wall, all of birds. Ato counted thirty in all.

"I told you Bello was a snake!" he declared.

A paper notice had been pasted on the rock beside the pictures.

SOMETIMES ALL YOU NEED IS A MOMENT TO COOL OFF, AND YOU WILL FIND THE WAY! it said in bold letters.

There was another message pasted beside it, printed in smaller letters:

> *Asafo observe all as they walk on life's road*
> *Eyes open, taking in all the beauty they're showed*
> *You saw twelve of these birds rowing from Lakeside here*
> *Now pick them off the wall, and head straight back there*

You win a point for every right bird you choose
But for every wrong one a point you will lose
Before you choose, take heed, pause, and think
Or you may end up with a face full of ink.

There was a moment of silence.

Hafsat slid a triumphant glance at Dzifa. "And you yelled at me for looking at the birds."

"I'm sorry," Dzifa grunted. "Can we just get this done?"

All four of them spotted the avocet. Leslie tugged the picture off the wall.

"I think we saw this," Dzifa said, and lifted off a picture of a short, fat bird with green feathers.

"Aaargh!" she squealed, as a thin jet of sticky yellow ink squirted onto her face.

After that, the rest of the choices were left to Ato, while Dzifa vainly tried to clean off sticky ink from her face and hands. One by one Ato picked off a cormorant, jacana, heron, sandpiper, tree duck, pratincole, pied kingfisher, stilt, moorhen, and crane.

Soon he had eleven pictures, with no inky mishaps. One more to go.

"Did we see those?" Leslie asked. He gestured to a bird with a long, pointed beak and black wings.

"A godwit. Hmm . . . I dunno. Maybe," Ato said. He lifted the picture away slowly and braced himself against the possible spray of ink. None came.

"Yes!" they exclaimed in exhalation.

With a whoop of joy, they rushed out of the cave, waving

to Richie, who at first yelled a cheerful, "Well done," before his expression turned quizzical.

"Where's Hafsat?" he asked.

Only then did the Gallant Geese notice that Hafsat was not with them.

They ran back into the cave, flashing the light around the small space. She wasn't there. They looked at each other worriedly. Where was Hafsat? No one had seen her slip away.

"Ato! Richieee!"

They ran outside again. Hafsat stood at the mouth of the cave, looking sheepish.

"Hafsat!" Richie barked. "You should stay with your team!"

Ato started. He had never heard Richie sound so much like Kai.

"I'm sorry," Hafsat said, slipping on her life jacket and scrambling aboard the raft. "I just went around to—"

"Move!" Richie barked, getting into his canoe.

Hafsat gave him a hurt look and began rowing.

"Hafsat, faster!" Dzifa urged as the raft floated out to deeper water. "We only have fifteen minutes to go."

"I'm rowing fast!" Hafsat protested.

"You're not."

"I am!"

"You don't know what fast means. You only understand stop and slow!"

"Fast doesn't mean everything, Dzifa," Hafsat replied indignantly. She dropped her oars and jumped to her feet in indignation. The raft tipped to one side. Richie called out a warning, but Hafsat had lost her balance. Her arms flailed about, reaching for Dzifa. Dzifa ducked sharply and Hafsat toppled backward. With a splash, she landed in the water and disappeared from sight. Leslie shrieked.

Ato leapt in after her. The water covered his head as he sank into its cloudy depths.

CHAPTER THIRTEEN

Buoyed by his life jacket, Ato bobbed back to the surface, coughing up lake water. Slimy weeds from the lake clung to his legs. Through stinging eyes, he saw Hafsat spluttering and thrashing beside him. Waterweeds trailed down her head. He blinked water out of his eyes. His lungs stung from inhaled water as Richie hauled him and Hafsat onto their raft.

Dzifa stared at her feet while Richie gave them a sound scolding.

"Dzifa, a crocodile could have eaten her up. Or some big fish, like Jonah and the whale," Leslie added unhelpfully.

"A whale? In lake water that came up to our chests?" Dzifa scoffed.

"You should at least sound sorry about this, Dzifa. Hafsat was scared," Richie chided. Dzifa mumbled a grudging apology.

Kai rowed up, looking hot and cross. Alongside their raft, she patted her hip for a water flask that wasn't there. Richie unhooked his from his belt and tossed it over to her. She took a long drink from it, listening disapprovingly to how Hafsat had fallen into the lake. Ato caught the look on Leslie's face while Kai quenched her thirst; Leslie did not approve of sharing cups, spoons, or any other germ transmitters.

Kai handed Richie back his flask, told them they had dropped a point, and ordered them back to Hillside.

"A whole point. I wish a crocodile *had* eaten her up," Dzifa whispered uncharitably to Ato as they rowed back. Both Leslie and Hafsat were seated at the back of the raft.

"You could at least say sorry to her."

"She fell into water, not acid. I'm not sorry. *She* should be sorry. She's lost us points for time."

"Be nice to her." Ato lowered his voice and glanced backward. "Her dad died, you know. That must be hard. She just doesn't want to talk about it." He spoke in a low tone, or so he thought.

"Oh no," Leslie exclaimed from behind. "Hafsat, your dad died? I'm so sorry!" There was genuine compassion in his voice.

"Leslie!" Ato hissed, darting a warning glance at him. He caught the reproachful look in Hafsat's eyes, and embarrassment washed over him.

"I'm sorry," he began. "I didn't . . ."

Hafsat looked away and kept rowing, keeping her eyes on the water.

"You should know when to shut up, Leslie!" Ato scolded quietly when they arrived back at Hillside and joined Flock Eleven at the Chirp and Chatter. They had arrived on shore with one minute to spare.

"*Leslie* should know when to shut up? That's strange, seeing that you blabbed first," Dzifa retorted.

"She doesn't want to talk about it!"

"Why?" Leslie looked thoughtful as they walked into the Chirp and Chatter. "*You* don't get upset when we talk about your dad."

The top three table was on the screen.

TEAM	MISSION FIVE: Points out of 125	POSITION OUT OF 16
Talented Turkeys	109	1st
Dynamic Doves	105	2nd
Gallant Geese	104	3rd

With five missions done and three to go, the Talented Turkeys had snatched back first place. The Dynamic Doves were in second place. Ato and his teammates were overjoyed to still be in third place, despite their dropped point. Many kids had inky faces, and apparently no other team had brought back all twelve birds *and* an intact raft *and* been on time.

On the list below, the Nifty Nightingales—who were already on cloud nine after having lunch with Eyra earlier that afternoon—were ecstatic to be in fifth position. The Brilliant Buzzards, having left the sixteenth position for number fourteen, hopped about in a spontaneous victory dance around the room.

Top three, Ato thought happily. What a great position to be in before their dinner with Eyra tonight!

◆ ◆ ◆ ◆ ◆ ◆ ◆

As they left the Chirp and Chatter to their cabins for Nest Rest, a new thought wormed its way into Ato's head. He was sure the plan was hidden at the top of the Dawn Locus, but he still wanted to go back to search the gentle valley that ran through Rockside. There were a couple of pretty good spots there to hide a plan. He had no desire for another nighttime encounter with a snake, so he formed a plan: sneak away by himself during Nest Rest, while the teams—and hopefully Guardians—were in their cabins napping. He would be back before Nest Rest was over, in time for games at the Flocking Valley and dinner with Eyra.

As Flock Eleven streamed toward their cabins, Ato pulled Leslie aside.

"If anyone asks, say I'm already in the cabin," he whispered. Before his hapless friend could protest, Ato had vanished through the dense brush.

Once at Rockside, he began his search, ducking and weaving underneath low, intertwined branches. He snagged his pants on a thorny bush and grazed his palms clambering over stony mounds. A safe place, his father had said.

He searched for hiding places in thick undergrowth and underneath prickly bushes. He hunted behind boulders and scared the rodents there. He startled a nesting bird in a tree hollow. It chased him off, beating angry wings about his head. Huge lizards in rock crevices sent him leaping backward, and rats jumped out at him from underneath rocks. A wasp stung him on his neck, and an army ant nipped his shin. He tripped and fell down a rocky outcrop and began scratching frenziedly when his skin brushed a hairy plant.

After nearly an hour, all he had to show for his efforts were a burning bump on his neck, a blister on his leg, and an itchy rash on his hand. Tired, thirsty, and disappointed, he sank beneath a shady tree, leaning back against its thick trunk. Leslie was right. Nnoma was a jungle.

If it wasn't down here, it had to be up at the peak, he thought wearily. Maybe he was wasting his time. Perhaps Eyra knew where he needed to look. In a few hours, he would have dinner with her and he would find out. It was a comforting thought. Worn out from his efforts, he closed his eyes. The cries of songbirds carried over the cooling air. His head drooped against his chest.

By the time he opened his eyes, the sun had dipped toward the western horizon beyond the lake, throwing a deep orange hue across the sky.

Dinner! Eyra!

He scrambled up and began to run, feet pounding the earth in rhythm with the blood in his ears. Was he too late?

As he rounded the crest toward the Flocking Valley, breathless and perspiring, a blur of skinny limbs flew at him.

"Where were you, Ato?" Dzifa exclaimed. "We looked for you everywhere!"

Leslie's face was polished to a shine, and Ato was aware of how he looked. He rubbed his filthy hands on his shorts. "Gosh, I'm so sorry," he panted. "I just—"

"You know the rules," Leslie scolded. "Teams stay together! Now we got points taken off. I told them you were in the cabin. And Richie climbed up to check!"

Dzifa waved him on impatiently. "Come on, let's go! Everyone is heading to dinner! Kai is *so* mad at us." She began running and halted, jabbing a finger at him. "You went looking for it!"

"I thought I'd have a quick look."

"A quick look?" Leslie looked as if he wanted to kick him. "Ato, this is an island, not your closet!"

Kai was striding toward them, her eyeballs almost popping out of their sockets in vexation. "Where were you, Ato? Eyra is already in the Pecking Bowl!"

"Just . . . just looking around." How could he have slept so long? What if Eyra did not want to meet them now? What if she got mad and left without them?

"You *cannot* go off by yourself. This is not a school playground. There are pits! Ravines! Birds that can rip your scalp off! You just lost your team a point. And look at you!"

Ato gulped in dismay. He was going to dinner with Eyra with grimy clothes and rips in his pants.

"Let's hope Eyra isn't cross with us," Leslie panted. "We'll be the only group who didn't get to eat with her because we were late. And dirty."

Kai hurried them up as Eyra, wearing a long yellow-and-blue wraparound dress, appeared in the doorway.

"There you are." She beamed, waving at them. "Let's go make the most of our evening together!"

Thank goodness, Ato thought. Eyra wasn't mad at them for being late. He gave a huge sigh of relief.

CHAPTER FOURTEEN

EYRA STEPPED BRISKLY INTO THE COOLING EVENING. SHE walked so fast that Ato had to skip across the uneven path to keep pace with her. "Thank you for coming to spend the evening with me, Gallant Geese," she said with a smile, turning to them.

On the way, Eyra asked questions about everything—school, home, their friends, and how they were finding Nnoma. She talked excitedly about joining them on the hike up the Dawn Locus and for the mountaintop picnic.

By the time they were climbing the stone steps that led to the wild garden just outside her tree cabin, Ato felt totally at ease. Two massive trees towered on opposite ends of the expanse of fruit trees, bushes, creepers, and flowers that made up the garden. Their interlocking branches formed a leafy ceiling. The garden stretched from her cabin on the right down to a rocky slope covered in brambles that dropped toward Woodside. Eyra settled them at a round wooden table in a corner beneath one of the giant trees. Five ceramic plates were set around it, with gourds for cups. "We only eat indoors if it rains," she explained.

From nowhere, a man appeared beside them. This must be the cook! Ato realized. He was a tall, thin man wearing dark glasses. His lips twitched as if he were muttering a silent prayer.

"Marko." Eyra smiled. He swiveled his head in their direction and nodded toward each of them. All the while, he rocked gently from side to side and tapped his fingertips lightly together.

"Welcome, young ones," he murmured. His voice was flat and unwelcoming. His face was expressionless.

"You may serve us, Marko," she said.

He nodded and padded off to an outdoor kitchen stand. His movement reminded Ato of a panther. He was soon back, balancing several platters, which he set on a nearby table. Then he slid out a glittering knife from his apron and got to work. They watched entranced as he pattered around the garden snatching fruits, tearing off leaves, tugging up roots. His steps were cat-like, silent, and velvety. Then he was dicing, slicing, and wielding his knife as if it were a baton in a street parade. He crushed seeds and tossed leaves, juggling several dishes at once on the outdoor hot plate. He was in perfect control. Once in a while he would stop moving and stand perfectly still . . . as though he were listening for something they could not hear or had caught the scent of something invisible.

"He knows everything by feel, taste, and smell," Eyra said to the impressed children. "He knows which plants here are good to eat and which ones should be left alone. Not all natural things are good for you, you see. Some are pretty to look at but should be left well alone."

Ato started as the cook appeared beside him. He hadn't heard the man approach. There was something creepy about Marko, Ato thought. He didn't think he'd want to be alone with him.

Eyra watched Ato, amusement lurking in her eyes. "Yes, Ato, Marko does have that effect on people. I think he enjoys it."

Ato squirmed, embarrassed. Had she guessed what he'd been thinking?

"I don't know what I would do without him. He knows what I need before I ask. That's his home right there." She pointed to a small bamboo bungalow on the opposite end of the garden, across from her cabin. "He sticks close to me."

Marko set platters before them—an attractive salad of leaves, edible flowers, and fruit. There were bowls of mixed roasted seeds, tender chunks of grilled river fish, vegetable sauce with a sweet, spicy fragrance, and a bowl of soft, steamed grains.

They began to eat. "What we choose to eat makes a huge difference to how the earth fares," Eyra said earnestly. "Here in Nnoma we hope you'll discover food that's tasty, good for you, doesn't cost a lot, and doesn't need to be brought to you on planes and ships. Some of these you might know, some you might not." She picked up the pretty salad and offered it to Ato.

"Try this. The topping is made from tree nuts."

Ato hesitantly crunched into the salad. To his surprise, it tasted delicious. Hafsat ate slowly, her eyes taking in Eyra's garden with its spectacular range of bushes and shrubs and flowers in colors from red, violet, and pink, to white and yellow.

"You have eyes that don't miss much, Hafsat," Eyra said, munching on a nut.

Hafsat gave her a bashful smile. "I love your garden, especially the flowers," she said.

"I love my flowers too." Eyra's eyes caressed her garden. "I love to smell them. Wear them. Drink them."

Leslie pulled a face. "Drink them?"

"Yes, Leslie. Petals of violets, roses, hibiscus, lavender—it depends on what's flowering. Marko steeps them in a gourd of warm water. He leaves it out here, covered with a napkin, before he goes to bed. At dawn before the birds start their chorus, before the sun rises, before I speak to anyone, I sit on my garden steps. Wrapped in my shawl, I sip my tonic, enriched with the fragrant goodness of the flowers, and listen to the dawn breeze whispering to me."

Hafsat's brown eyes were filled with curiosity. "What does it whisper?"

"Good ideas. For Nnoma, and for our world." Her eyes twinkled. "But I'm not always alone. The creatures of the night keep me company. I often see bush babies playing, leaping about with their huge eyes and ears." Her eyes took on a thoughtful look. "Sometimes, though, I hear other sounds in my garden, and I wonder whether those are bush babies."

"I nearly got to see one on our first mission," Dzifa said. Her face fell. "But I missed it. Can I come here at dawn to see one?"

Eyra nodded. "Of course you may. So long as it's the whole team. You might find them leaping about like mini-kangaroos. Playing like children. And they cry like babies. But you'll have to get out of bed very, very early to do that."

After dinner they sat back, sipping Marko's spicy sweet hibiscus-and-ginger cordial while he silently cleared up the table.

Eyra took Ato's hand and stroked it, looking into his eyes. "A bag of energy, that's what you are, Ato. A hunter. You don't stop until you have what you want. You remind me of . . ." She paused. "A falcon."

"Wow! My favorite bird!"

"I'm not surprised," she said. "Just like a falcon, you fix your eye on the best way to reach your goal. Like your dad." Her tone softened. "He was the kind who simply did what needed to be done. No excuses."

Ato sat up. This was his cue! "Eyra, what else do you know about my dad? Did he tell you anything about . . . a plan?"

"Your dad." A wistful smile spread across Eyra's face. "What a wonderful man he was! Made friends everywhere he went. I called him the Dream-Seeder because he had a way of dropping great ideas into my mind the way one drops seeds into a flower bed. And as seeds grow into flowers, the words he spoke to me grew into a dream, a dream that I worked at until it became reality." She patted Ato's hand. "He had a gift; he could encourage people to do more than they thought they could!" She sighed. "I miss him. I'm sure his whole family does too."

Ato could have melted with pride.

"But you talk of a plan . . ." Eyra scratched her chin with a slender finger. "Let me see . . ."

Ato exchanged eager glances with his teammates.

"I remember one afternoon so well," she continued. "It had

been a difficult day planning a path up to the Dawn Locus. Your father and I sat on the hillside facing the lake. We drank fresh coconut water and talked about how we wanted to heal the world.

"Then your father told me something. He said, *Eyra, when there's something to be done, we worry about whether people will know what to do. My son is a baby; I keep feeling that I need to write instructions for every fix he'll find himself in.*"

Eyra maintained her hold on Ato's hand. "I remember the lines on your father's forehead deepened. They always did when he was thinking hard. Then he said, *If my son's in a fix and I'm not here, Eyra, I hope he'll find the directions were with him all along. Not written in ink. But inside—stamped on his heart.*"

"There was something more that he said . . ." Eyra said in a whisper.

But suddenly her eyelids fluttered down, hiding her eyes. In that split second, a look crossed her face, one that Ato recognized.

Fear.

When she looked up, her eyes were bright and dancing again. "Never mind," she said cheerfully.

Ato's shoulders drooped. "But . . . you were going to say something."

"That something can wait, Ato." Her voice was light but firm.

The moment was gone. Ato swallowed his disappointment as Eyra turned to Dzifa.

"The warrior," she said, and smiled.

"The magpie," Ato muttered.

Dzifa flashed Ato an indignant look.

Eyra raised a delicate black eyebrow. "A very intelligent bird. Bold. Not afraid to speak your mind."

Ato's feelings must have shown on his face, because Eyra's nose twitched in amusement.

"You know that all too well, don't you, Ato?"

He scowled.

Eyra's eyes turned back to Dzifa. "Yes, Dzifa, you struggle to act nice when you don't feel nice. You're brave enough to leave the pack; it doesn't matter what Ato thinks and if Leslie won't come along. You'll go alone. Am I right?"

Dzifa's lips parted in surprise and she nodded, looking lost for words.

Eyra turned to Ato. "You do know that she does this because she has to be true to herself. She can't follow the crowd if their chants ring in her ears but not in her heart." She took Dzifa's hands so that their fingers were interlaced. "And your friends can trust you. In time, you will learn to put yourself in another person's shoes and be able to feel what they feel."

"I will?" she asked, sounding surprised. "'Cos I don't get people. At all."

"Trust me." Eyra smiled.

Dzifa nodded slowly, looking thoughtful, as Eyra let go of her hands.

"And now Leslie—"

"Leslie's the parakeet," Ato teased.

"I just like to be safe," Leslie said earnestly. "My mum says Dzifa is wild and Ato is reckless."

Eyra laughed. "You're special, Leslie. You don't need to be like anyone else. You don't need to say sorry about who you are." She turned her dancing gaze to his friends. "He doesn't mind being the only one missing the party, does he?"

Despite himself, Ato laughed. "Not even if the whole school is going."

"It's a strength not to be afraid to have a different opinion, Leslie, even if it makes you less popular." She looked intently at them. "I'm not always popular. I have heard whispers, things about Nnoma that people want done differently. But their reasons are for the good of just a few people, not for the good of all people." Her expression sobered. "I won't have that. I too have a different opinion: Nnoma is for the world. That's the dream. But not everyone agrees with that."

Ato exchanged puzzled looks with his friends. He could see they didn't understand Eyra either.

Eyra had turned to Hafsat.

"I see a girl who wants things to stay the same—steady and beautiful. But just like a boat on the sea, we all get rocked by choppy water." She touched Hafsat's stomach. "You feel it here, don't you, when things get rough?"

Hafsat nodded, eyes wide.

"Hafsat, you think you are weak, and you yearn for friends. But remember this: Your friends need you too, even if they don't know. You want to run away from hard situations, but you have to face them. And you'll find that you are stronger than you thought you were."

To Ato's utter surprise, and the clear bewilderment of the other two, tears slid down Hafsat's face. Eyra slid over and wrapped her in a tender embrace, murmuring soothing sounds.

Still holding Hafsat close, Eyra looked over at Ato and his friends.

"Gallant Geese, I know you don't see it, but I'll tell you this—together, you've got everything needed to be a winning team, and that doesn't always mean becoming an Asafo. You're each different from the other, and that's what makes you strong. Together, that makes you a perfect whole."

Ato felt confused. Why was Hafsat crying? And what was it that Eyra had started to say earlier? He desperately wanted to ask her more, especially about the plan or anything more his father had said. But then would she think that he was only here to find answers for his questions? That he didn't care about Nnoma itself? That he didn't want to be a protector of the earth? Maybe he had to tell her that the plan was about saving Nnoma, he thought.

Eyra let go of Hafsat. The girl dabbed her eyes, sniffled, and gave Eyra a watery smile. "Thank you," she whispered.

"Ato has something to ask me," she murmured, her eyes holding his. "But it must be another time. I promise you—we'll make time to speak again before you leave Nnoma."

Ato's lips parted in surprise. He broke into an uncertain smile. "Thank you, Eyra."

"And I can come here again too?" Dzifa asked, her eyes flicking from Hafsat to Eyra in curiosity. "To see the bush babies?"

"Yes, you too, Dzifa. My garden is always open to you. While you are here, we have to make the most of our time together."

Ato felt a wave of satisfaction. He would grab a chance to talk to Eyra as soon as he could. As early as the next day, Saturday.

CHAPTER FIFTEEN

As usual, Eyra was at breakfast the following morning, this time in a purple dress that reminded Ato of an emperor butterfly's wings. During the hop-cross-skip dance that she led them in, Ato kept trying to skip close to her. It was hard. Scores of hyped-up kids had the same idea. For his efforts, he earned a stamp on his little toe from a Lively Lark and an elbow in his ribs from a Talented Turkey. After an unintentional poke on the nose from a fourteen-year-old Dynamic Dove with a mustache, he gave up.

Trying to get Eyra alone was a different level of tricky, he thought. He was annoyed with himself for not getting Eyra to tell him exactly when they could speak. He watched her dance out of the hall with the Super Swifts and crossed his fingers. Hopefully he *would* get to see her today. And maybe, just maybe, she would have something to say that would help him find the plan.

Two hours later he was out in the sunshine with the rest of Flock Eleven at the Flocking Valley for a morning of fun games before Mission Six in the afternoon. Throughout the games, as birds wheeled and shrieked in the clear skies above, and kids screamed with excitement around him, Ato's mind roamed from becoming an Asafo to the plan, and to what Eyra was hiding from him. He felt muddled and a little anxious, but he knew just who to talk to.

Toward the end of the games, he asked Frank the Tank for permission to make a phone call. Permission granted, he walked up the tree-shaded path to the Chirp and Chatter. Clara, the girl there who handled the phones, was watching dancing horses on the huge TV. She looked barely older than some of the Flock Eleven kids. Maybe eighteen years old, he figured.

"I need to talk to my grandmother, please," he said.

With a smile, she handed him a phone. He tapped out a number and held the slim device to his ear. The number was busy. He tried twice more. Still busy. Clara noticed his frustration.

She gave him a sympathetic look. "Let's give her a few minutes."

He handed the phone back and wandered over to the window at the other end of the room. The lake reflected bronze in the sunlight, and a wave of heat hit his face. He took a step back behind the door where a pile of floor cushions had been stacked. Here, he was shielded from the heat, but still had a clear view of the water.

"Ato?" Clara sounded puzzled.

He stepped out from behind the door.

"Oh, you were invisible, behind that door." She laughed, handing him the phone. "For a moment there, I thought you had gone. Here, I made your call."

Ato raised the phone to his ear. "Nana!"

"It's been four days and I don't know how I'm going to find it," he admitted when Nana asked how he was getting on. He sank onto the colored floor cushions "The island is amazing, but . . ." His voice trailed off miserably.

"But you think you'll have failed if you don't become an Asafo or find the plan?"

"Yeah. But we're always so busy. If I—we—could find the plan, or become Asafo, I'd be happy. I think I'd rather find the plan. Oh, I don't know. Which is better, Nana?"

There was a pause.

"Ato," Nana said softly. "Why do you have teeth?"

He hesitated. "To chew?"

"Why do you have legs?"

"To walk?" Why was she asking him these questions?

"Now shut your eyes."

He obeyed. Everything went dark despite the bright sunshine outside.

"Picture your favorite bird."

At once he saw it: a clear sky, a distinctive shadow hovering high. Then a shooting blur as with wings folded back the peregrine falcon plummeted at blinding speed toward its prey. A smile crept across his face.

"You can see that peregrine falcon even when it's not actually there, can't you, Ato? Now keep your eyes closed. What do you want most?"

His smile spread wider. He could see an old sheet of paper in his hands. The writing on it was his father's.

"And just the same way you have teeth and your legs, there's a reason you have that power," Nana said softly.

"What power, Nana?"

"The power to see what you want even when you don't actually have it. Trust that power, Ato. Say thank you for it. Then go ahead and enjoy your stay on Nnoma. Be a good teammate. Be a good friend. It's okay to think about what you want. But think too about what would be good for everyone. That's what's best. Because you too are a part of 'everyone.'"

The call ended a few minutes later and Ato was soon heading back down the hillside to join the laughing children coming back up to lunch. Somewhere up a nearby tree, a parrot's chuckle filtered through the branches to his ears. He hoped he would soon have something to chuckle about too. He wanted to become an Asafo *and* to find the plan for Nnoma. Nana had spoken about what would be good for everyone. What was that? Finding the plan? Or becoming an Asafo? He didn't know the answer.

CHAPTER SIXTEEN

EYRA DID NOT SHOW UP AT THE PECKING BOWL FOR LUNCH that Saturday. There was surprise and disappointment on the faces of Flock Eleven. The Gallant Geese kept twisting their necks around like turkeys watching the empty doorway. The Splendid Sandpipers, whose turn it was to lunch with Eyra, stood by their table fidgeting while they waited.

"Settle down, Flock Eleven," the Guardians urged. Eyra was busy, they said. She would show up soon. Richie was not at lunch either. Ato missed his jokes at their table. He figured Richie would be helping Eyra, but he hoped they would finish quickly so Eyra would come to lunch.

Lunch was a mouthwatering spread of stuffed vegetables, stews, and herby cooked grains. But even the sweet tiger nut pudding did nothing to make Ato feel better. By the time lunch was over, one of the Splendid Sandpipers, a tiny eleven-year-old with huge eyes, was in tears. Koku went over to her.

"Eyra will make it up to you," he said. "The wait will be worth it when you get to eat with her."

This did not make the now Sorry Sandpipers feel better. "There's only one chance for each team to eat alone with Eyra. Now we'll have to join another group. And it won't be so—so special," the tiny Sandpiper sniffed.

The Guardians tried to raise the spirits in the room with songs and jokes. They were not successful. No one could be Eyra, Ato realized.

Kai looked watchful and nervous. Her eyes darted around like a lizard's. She licked her lips and muttered to herself. Maybe she had missed Richie too, Ato thought.

During Nest Rest that afternoon, Ato drifted into sleep, worn out by the morning's activities. He was horrified to find himself flailing about in the lake, struggling to keep above water. And there was a still form beneath him, on the murky lake bed: Hafsat. He stretched an arm to save her, but she was out of reach. Stand up, he tried to call to her, it's only waist-deep. But lake water gurgled down his throat, choking him.

The swirling water raised mud from the lake bed, making it hard to see anything. He reached for her, but his fingers touched only turbulent water. The current was carrying her away! While he tried to save Hafsat, Dzifa stood on the edge of the lake watching with an un-sorry look on her face, while Leslie flapped hysterically, parakeet-style.

A gentle tinkling woke him up and he sprang to a sitting position. Nest Rest was over. It was time for Mission Six.

Richie was already at the Flocking Valley when the Gallant Geese arrived. Ato was pleased to be finally sitting on the seat with the falcon etching, but he still complained to Richie about their disappointment when Eyra hadn't shown up for lunch.

Richie seemed preoccupied with his thoughts. He patted Ato's shoulder absentmindedly. "Sorry about that. Eyra's been busy. You'll see her soon." He indicated to Ato to be quiet as Kai's voice rang out with brief instructions for Mission Six.

"Find your Asafo principle in the Nursery Rhyme Hunt and be back here in ninety minutes. Please walk along the laid-out paths when you're coming back." Then she handed each team a note. The Gallant Geese's read:

Your starting point is Rockside, underneath the meeting point for nature's cleanup crew.

"Nature's cleanup crew?" Leslie looked confused.

Bello and his team had figured out the clue for their starting point and gone running off. "Falcons take off faster than geese do," he called goadingly to Ato as he left.

Ato stuck out his tongue at Bello's back. "We've got to guess what that is, quickly," he fretted. At that moment, it hit him. "Vultures!" he yelled.

They scurried along Hillside, down the wooded side of the island that lay west of the Dawn Locus, and to Rockside, where spiky plants and boulders stretched down to the lake. Thick bushes grew around the rocks, along with bunches of grass with pink stalks that drooped downward, together looking like a head of hair.

Hafsat pointed at plants dangling from tree trunks and branches. "I have . . . I had these growing on the wall in my garden," she said. "They don't grow on the ground. They get their food and water from the air around the wall."

"That's like being a parasite," Dzifa said.

"It's not," Hafsat objected. "Parasites suck life out. These are epiphytes. That's what my dad tells . . . told me. The just live on walls and trees. It's like having a friend to lean on."

"That's annoying—a friend leaning *all* the time." Dzifa looked pointedly at Hafsat.

Hafsat pouted. "Are you telling me something?"

"We're here, what next?" Ato interrupted. They had arrived beneath a tall tree with a committee of vultures hunched on its highest branches.

"They look hungry. I'll bet they're asking themselves: Who's dying today?" Dzifa remarked.

"Must be hard. Born ugly and having to eat rotting animals," Leslie said, wrinkling his nose.

"Someone's got to clean up," Dzifa said.

Beneath the tree was a rectangular wooden board. They inspected it curiously. On either end of the board were two square pieces of wood. One of them had a U-shaped piece of metal attached to it. There were two small holes, like eyes, on either end of the U. On the other piece of wood was a small metal square, attached to the wood by thick string. In the center of the board, a small metal prong the size of a match rested on a paper note. The note was headed *GALLANT GEESE*. Below the heading, in simple black print were the words:

One, two . . .

Ato flicked away a trickle of perspiration from his temple. "One, two . . . what?"

Dzifa traced the U-shaped piece of metal with her finger. "This looks like a horseshoe," she said.

"It does," Ato agreed. He picked up the slim metal prong. "Do you think this teeny thing would fit here?" He slid it through the holes on either end of the U-shaped metal. It fit perfectly.

"Now it looks like a buckle," Leslie observed

"Remember the nursery rhyme," Hafsat said, still staring at the note. "One, two . . ."

" . . . buckle my shoe!" Ato, Dzifa, and Leslie exclaimed in unison.

"That's it! Oh my gosh! That's it!" Hafsat sang happily. "My dad always says . . . always said that the first thing you think of is usually correct!"

They moved the two wooden squares together to buckle the horseshoe. Revealed on the board, on the space that the two squares had initially covered, was an inked inscription:

Two hundred paces west, where the hornbill sleeps.

"West is that way!" Dzifa pointed in the direction of the lake. Hastily, they counted their steps in the direction of the afternoon sun.

"It will be an old tree. With a hollow!" Ato said.

He was right. Exactly two hundred paces west, a gnarled tree, tall and naked, stood amid the rocks and thorny bushes. At eye level on its trunk was a hollow. Beside the hollow a miniature door hung open.

"Three, four, shut the door!" they chorused. Up in the tree, a purple macaw screeched down rudely at them.

They swung it shut, and found a note on the trunk behind it, pinned to the knobbly bark. *Head south, where the fruity medicine tree grows*, it directed. Still, Ato peered inside the hollow hopefully. Apart from a couple of fuzzy green-and-black caterpillars, there was nothing.

Following the note's instructions, they ran another five minutes south to a guava tree, behind which lay a loose bundle of sticks.

"Five, six, pick up sticks!" they chanted.

A letter of the alphabet had been painted on each stick.

"Lay them straight!" they sang.

The message on the rearranged sticks led them to a thorny bush. Behind it, a toy hen sat on an envelope. Opening the envelope, the Gallant Geese found a printed note: *The Asafo finds meaning in the circle of nature, and understands that in nature, one thing always leads to another. Nothing stands on its own.*

Carrying off their Asafo principle in triumph, the Gallant Geese tramped back toward the Flocking Valley merrily singing their rhyme:

> *One, two, buckle my shoe,*
> *Three, four, shut the door,*
> *Five, six, pick up sticks,*
> *Seven, eight, lay them straight,*
> *Nine, ten, a big fat hen.*

The fifth time they began the rhyme, Ato glanced at his watch.

The Flocking Valley was a good ten-minute walk along the main path. But . . .

"Look." He pointed toward a giant aloe plant that grew nearly ten feet high and almost as wide. It was about one hundred yards away from the path. "All we need to do is cross that patch of ground where the aloe is, and we'll be at the Flocking Valley. We could earn points for getting back early. We could even beat the Falcons."

Leslie scanned the terrain as if they were on a big-cat safari. "Kai won't like it if we take a different route."

"Kai's not here," Ato cut in. "And going my way will chop off at least five minutes."

"We'd have to climb over those first," Hafsat said doubtfully, eyeing an outcrop of rocks jutting out between them and the giant aloe. "My dad always says . . . always said not to take unnecessary risks."

"Those rocks look risky," Leslie said. He cast a longing glance back in the opposite direction.

"Those rocks are no problem," Dzifa said, following Ato along the stony course leading to the rocks. "Let's get some points!"

Leslie trudged behind her muttering about reckless people. Hafsat trailed at the back looking at clusters of tiny purple flowers that grew in bright contrast to the green moss on the rocks.

They made it successfully over the rocks, past thorny bushes, and around the formidable aloe. Behind it, a weather-beaten wooden board lay on the ground across their path.

"Should we walk over it? Or jump? Oh, you know what?"

A thought flashed through Ato's head. "It could be covering something!"

His friends looked doubtfully at the board when he shared his thought.

"Why would your dad hide a plan here?" Hafsat wondered.

"Come on, guys, help me lift it," Ato said. He knew he absolutely had to look.

Together the Gallant Geese grasped one end of the board and strained to lift it. It seemed stuck to the ground.

"Harder," Ato urged. Leslie gave a dramatic sigh. When they had lifted the board a couple of feet above the ground, Ato found himself looking down into a V-shaped rock pit. It was about three feet across its mouth, and seven or eight feet deep.

Bugs, beetles, and insects scuttled into view, confused by the light. Soft moss grew over the rock face all the way to the bottom of the pit, where a heap of moldering vegetation let off a dank smell.

A cockroach scuttled up the board . . . toward Leslie's fingers. He squealed and let go.

"Hey!" Ato tried to grab the plank, but it was too late. With a grating thump, the board slid over the edge, landing at the bottom of the pit. Ato groaned. Now there was a deep pit in front of them, a jagged rock face on their left, and a thick prickly bush on their right.

"It's a sign," Leslie declared. "We're not supposed to be here. We should go back."

"Let's jump across," Ato said impulsively. "It's easy—look!" And with a running jump he sailed across the three-foot opening.

"Me next. One, two, threeee!" With the agility of a grasshopper, Dzifa sprang across the hole with a couple of feet to spare.

"This is how trips turn to tragedies," Leslie warned. Nonetheless, he cleared the hole comfortably, landing on his feet on the other side.

"Come on, Hafsat," Ato called. "Just count one-two-three . . . and then over!" He paused.

Hafsat took a couple of steps toward the hole and lurched forward. She did not have enough momentum and landed right on the edge on the other side. For a millisecond, it looked like she had made it. Then, with a shriek, she slipped down into the hole.

CHAPTER SEVENTEEN

Hafsat burst into tears.

"Oh, for heaven's sake! You should have said you couldn't jump!" Dzifa exclaimed, stamping her foot in exasperation.

"Have you broken anything?" Leslie called into the mossy pit in a panic. "Can you breathe? Are you bleeding?"

Ato broke out in a nervous sweat. Leslie was falling apart. Hafsat was bawling down in the pit. Maybe she had hurt herself. Badly. Dzifa looked so cross with Hafsat that he thought she might chuck a stone down at her.

"Everyone shush! Just shush for a minute!" He looked down anxiously at his crying teammate. "Are you okay, Hafsat?"

Dzifa waved him aside. "Of course she's okay. If she wasn't, she wouldn't be yelling so loudly. It's not that deep, let's get her out."

"Ourselves?" Leslie looked as if she had asked them to haul an elephant out of concrete. "Let's call Richie."

"And lose points?" Dzifa asked crossly. "No Guardians."

The rescue operation began. Ato stretched himself stomach-down on the rough ground and extended his arms into the pit.

Leslie sat on his back to keep him pinned down. A tearful Hafsat reached up to grasp Ato's wrists. She tried to heave herself upward, but her hands were too sweaty and she slipped back down.

"Try again," Ato panted. She hopped up and grabbed his wrists. But she began to slip back, unable to pull up her own body weight. Before her grasp gave way again, Dzifa sat herself astride Ato's upper back, reached over his head, and grasped Hafsat's arms. With Leslie anchoring her from behind, she heaved backward. Hafsat scrambled up the rest of the way and collapsed in a heap on top of her teammates. They picked themselves up and began running toward the Flocking Valley.

"Imagine messing up that easy jump!" Dzifa panted to Ato. Hafsat and Leslie were a few steps behind them.

Ato heard Leslie breathlessly ask Hafsat again how she was feeling. "You could have internal bleeding," he huffed. "I have an auntie who fell from a ladder. She climbed it to shoo her neighbor's cat from her roof. Everyone thought it was just a fall and then she began throwing up blood. The doctor said she was bleeding on the inside and if she hadn't come in then she would have died. My mother said it was the cat's revenge. Do you want to throw up?"

Behind Ato, Hafsat gave a choking sob. "My leg hurts. That's why my dad always says . . . always said I shouldn't follow the crowd." She sniffled loudly.

The lake and woods came into view, then the heads of the other kids at the Flocking Valley. The setting sun had turned the sky multiple shades of orange.

Kai watched them approaching. She eyed Hafsat's teary, scratched face and soiled clothes with suspicion.

"What happened, Hafsat?" she asked.

Hafsat dabbed her eyes with a dirty hand and began sobbing again.

"Richieee!" Kai called.

Richie strode over. He took one look at Kai's exasperated face and handed her his flask. She took a long swallow.

To Ato's relief, Hafsat did not say exactly what had happened. Richie assumed someone had been mean to her and he addressed the remaining three of them briskly about the importance of kindness to each other. When he was done, the Gallant Geese settled down at the Flocking Valley. Ato sat on a seat with a pelican etching. Leslie sat next to Hafsat, examining a graze on his arm and wondering aloud whether it could turn gangrenous.

The last few teams were running back. From what Ato overheard, several teams had struggled to make sense of their clues and had been unable to complete their missions. Ato was delighted to see that the Fantastic Falcons were one of the last teams to make it back to the Flocking Valley. Bello scowled and looked away when he saw Ato.

Ten minutes later, the top three table was up:

TEAM	MISSION SIX: Points out of 150	POSITION OUT OF 16
Talented Turkeys	128	1st
Gallant Geese	126	2nd
Excellent Eagles	125	3rd

Yes! Leslie, Dzifa, and Ato exclaimed, jumping up and hugging each other. Hafsat did not react. She sat twiddling her fingers and sniffling. Dzifa slid an unsympathetic glance at her.

"Ato, something about Hafsat doesn't add up," she whispered to him and Leslie a few minutes later. They were heading up the grassy hill toward the Pecking Bowl along with the rest of Flock Eleven. Hafsat trailed behind everyone else.

"Really? What?" Ato asked.

"Her dad. Sometimes she speaks as if he's alive. Then as if he's not. Past tense. Present tense. Past tense. It's confusing. What do you think?"

Leslie switched his attention from his possibly gangrenous arm to Hafsat.

Ato didn't know what to think.

"I'm going to ask her. It bugs me," Dzifa said. She turned around and walked back toward Hafsat.

He hurried after her and tugged at her arm. "No," he hissed. But she just pulled him along.

Hafsat slowed to a stop when she saw them. Dried tears marked her face.

"Hafsat." Dzifa turned a puzzled gaze on her.

Ato nudged Dzifa. "Don't!" he whispered fiercely.

A few kids who had gone ahead looked back with mild interest.

"It's nothing," Ato cut in hastily, but Dzifa would not be stopped.

"I don't understand. About your dad . . . I know he's dead, and I'm sorry about that . . . but . . ." she began.

Hafsat froze. Her lower lip wobbled and she looked accusingly at Ato.

"It's just a question. I get confused . . ." Dzifa continued.

"My dad isn't dead," Hafsat said. Her voice was almost too low to hear. "He's . . . in prison."

❖ ❖ ❖ ❖ ❖ ❖ ❖

That evening in the Pecking Bowl, Eyra wasn't at dinner. Ato chewed his food without tasting it.

Hafsat had asked permission to skip dinner and go straight to the cabin she shared with Dzifa.

Dzifa, who was mad at him.

"You care more about her than being friends with me," she'd said, and had proceeded to ignore him through dinner.

Leslie irritated him by wondering aloud what Hafsat's father had done.

"Do you think he did something awful?" he whispered to Ato, trying to hide his lips behind a napkin. "Why didn't she just tell you the truth?"

"Sometimes it's hard to tell people the whole truth, Leslie. Like whether you brought pepper spray," he had answered.

Leslie had the grace to look ashamed. Ato ate the rest of his meal in silence. He felt mystified by Hafsat. Why had she said her father was dead when he wasn't? *I know what that feels like,* she had said to him when he said he wished his father were here. That wasn't true.

Then something dawned on him. Hafsat had never actually said her father was dead. *He* had. And she hadn't said yes to that. She'd just said she didn't want to talk about it. He gave an inward groan. He hadn't been totally fair to Hafsat. He sighed. There was so much to think about. But for now he had to focus on the one important thing.

CHAPTER EIGHTEEN

THE NEXT MORNING WAS SUNDAY, AND WHILE NNOMA WAS still shrouded in darkness, Ato shook Leslie hard. His friend lay asleep, spread-eagled, mouth open, one arm dangling down the side of his lower bunk. Outside, the island's birds were already in fine form with their dawn chorus, but Leslie always slept right through. Trying to wake his friend was like trying to shift a bag of cement. Eventually Leslie's eyes sleepily fluttered open.

"What?" He blinked from the glare of the pencil flashlight Ato shone on his face. Disbelief reflected in his eyes as Ato told him what he had in mind.

"What? No! We should not go to Eyra's!" he groaned.

"We have to! Just for a minute. It's dawn—she'll be in her garden. She said so!"

"We've gotten into enough trouble already being where we're not supposed to be. No more, Ato. No more having a look and all that. We're climbing the Dawn Locus today. We should be asleep now!" He pulled his sheet over his face as if hoping that would make Ato vanish.

Ato sat on Leslie's chest and tugged the sheet from his face. "We only have three days left on Nnoma. And this is probably the best time to speak to Eyra. Remember she said she wakes up before the birds and sits in her garden? And she promised she would see me again to tell me something my dad told her! She won't mind us coming, I'm sure! If you won't come with me, I'll go by myself."

"You always do this, Ato," Leslie fretted. "I want to stay here and sleep, but I don't know what crazy thing you're going to do, and then I'll be in trouble for not stopping you. I have a bad feeling about this."

"You don't need to do anything. Just look out for me." He slid off Leslie's chest and began to dress.

"'Look out.'" The words were a trigger to Leslie. "Do you remember what happened the last time I was looking out for you?"

Ato remembered all too well. Leslie had been their lookout when he and Dzifa had broken into the Prophet of Fire's office back home. That break-in was on the list of the top five things he wanted to forget. Even though everything had worked out well later on, the memory gave him an instant tummy ache. By now he was dressed, and began pulling away Leslie's bedcovers.

With a grunt of frustration, Leslie slid out of bed and began pulling on his clothes in the semidarkness. "I guess I'll have to come with you. People will ask me questions and I won't know what to say 'cos we're supposed to be each other's keepers and all that. What if some vulture pecks out your eye in the dark? Hmm? What would you do?"

Together they stole down the rungs of their tree into the cool dawn air. But a surprise awaited them on the ground.

Dzifa was already there, standing in the dimness and wreathed in mist from the forest floor.

Leslie staggered backward. "Sheesh! I thought you were a ghost. What are you doing here?"

"Leslie!" She groaned, dropping her arm that held the camera. "There were two bush babies! Right there! Now you've driven them off!"

Leslie looked around nervously. "Ato's sneaking to Eyra's house where he has no business. We've got to stop him."

Dzifa considered them in the gloom. "Actually," she said airily, hooking her camera strap around her neck, "I was thinking of going to Eyra myself. To look for bush babies, not because you're going," she shot at Ato. "I don't care where you're going."

"The Prophet was right. You guys are possessed," Leslie said in a tone of defeat.

Ato was half relieved that Dzifa wanted to come. "Maybe we can—"

"I'm not talking to you, Ato. You have a new best friend. Go talk to her."

"And here she is," Leslie said.

Hafsat was gingerly making her way down her cabin rungs to them. "I saw you leave, Dzifa, and I heard voices . . ." Her voice trailed off.

"Hafsat, we've got to go with them," Leslie said. "You can't trust Dzifa and Ato on their own."

Ato was soon stealing away in the foggy dawn toward Eyra's, with his team behind him. The cool air felt like a damp scarf lightly brushing over his face. Everything was still and silent. Everything apart from Leslie, who trailed at the back with Hafsat.

"We're *only* looking to see if Eyra is in her garden." His voice was heavy with misgiving as they crept along. "That's always how it starts with Ato and Dzifa. *Only* looking. Next thing you know, we're getting arrested for breaking-and-entering."

Ato brushed away an invisible cobweb clinging to his face. "We weren't arrested. We got caught. Two different things."

"All I'm saying is we should watch these two," Leslie muttered to Hafsat. "They're demon-possessed, and Ato never got his deliverance, so he's still got a devil in him making him do stuff like this."

"What is he talking about?" Hafsat asked from the back of the team.

"It's a long story," Ato said hastily.

"It's a short story," Leslie snapped. "Ato and Dzifa broke into a very important man's office. And got caught. We could have been in real trouble. We could have gone to jail."

Hafsat gave a small whimper.

"But instead we found out he was an awful man," Ato continued doggedly. "He was doing horrible things to our community. The police took him away after that. So it turned out we did the right thing. And that's how we got to Nnoma."

Defeated, Leslie fell silent.

Soon enough, they arrived below the steps that led to Eyra's garden. Her cabin loomed above them, but Eyra was not on the steps.

"I thought we'd find her sitting here drinking her petal potion." Ato's voice was heavy with disappointment. "She said she was always here at dawn."

They crouched behind a taami bush and peered at the shadowy outlines of her garden.

"Perhaps she's in that shed," Ato murmured hopefully. Keeping low, he stole back around the lower grounds that surrounded her garden, all the way up to a lonely storage hut that stood a distance away. The hut was empty except for a few boxes and small bins. He hurried back to the steps.

"Fine. Let's go now." Leslie began to creep away.

Ato grasped his T-shirt, restraining him. "Let's wait a bit, maybe she'll come out."

The Geese remained as still as possible. Mosquitoes, drawn to their warm bodies, buzzed about their arms and faces and began to bite. Savagely. Leslie and Hafsat squirmed and slapped at their skin.

Ato nudged Leslie harder than was necessary. "Quiet."

"Oh, I see. You'd like them to just keep biting me? So I end up with malaria?"

Dzifa straightened up, scratching her arms. "I say we go up and find her."

Ato held her wrist. "We can't just walk up through the front. If there's someone watching we'll be shooed away."

"We can't stay here either. Look." She pointed to the eastern sky, where a faint streak of pink had appeared. A clutch of birds in a nearby tree chirruped. There was little time to spare.

"You're right," Ato said. Their time on Nnoma would soon be up, he thought uneasily. What if Eyra was busy and out of sight every day until they left? He studied the garden for a few more seconds. "Let's get closer."

"No, no, we can't get closer," Leslie hissed.

"How are we supposed to see, then? Maybe you should pass us the X-ray glasses you don't have," Dzifa said.

Ato considered their situation once more. Courage began to seep into him. Eyra *would* be glad to see him. There was nothing to be afraid of. "Maybe she's sitting at her table *inside* her cabin. Dzifa and I will go closer to see. Leslie, you stay here with Hafsat. We'll be back."

"That's what you said the last time," Leslie muttered.

Leaving Hafsat and Leslie behind the bush, Ato and Dzifa stole along the rough stone edge of the garden steps. They scuttled around the fringes of the yard behind shrubs and dwarf palms till they got to the bottom of the garden, where they had sat to eat with Eyra. There was something on the table. Ato looked closer. A gourd, covered with a napkin—her tonic. Ato gripped Dzifa's hand. They froze. Eyra was not there. But someone else was.

Right in the corner, almost hidden by the creeping plants that hung in heavy tendrils from the tree, was the unmistakable form of a person. Through the light dawn mist, the outline of a tall person could clearly be seen.

Then behind them there was a sound. They whirled around. Eyra. She stood perfectly still in the dawn gloom. Her face was half obscured by shadow, but it was Eyra, all right.

"Who are you?" she asked coldly.

CHAPTER NINETEEN

ATO FROZE. THIS WAS NOT THE EYRA HE KNEW. HER VOICE was emotionless. No warmth. No life.

Maybe she wasn't a morning person.

He gulped. "It's . . . Ato. And Dzifa."

"Ato and Dzifa," she repeated flatly.

Ato was confused. What was wrong with her, standing there like a zombie?

From the corner of his eye, he caught a tiny movement. The person lurking in the shadows! A band of fear circled his stomach and he clutched Dzifa's hand. Whoever it was didn't want to be seen.

Eyra was walking stiffly toward them.

Ato took a couple of steps back with Dzifa. They were getting closer to the mysterious figure!

"Ato and Dzifa," Eyra repeated, her voice still dull and cold.

She was mad at them, Ato thought. They should never have come here. She was walking toward them and they were being cornered.

"I . . . we're sorry, Eyra . . ." He couldn't stop his hands from shaking.

"We shouldn't have . . ." Dzifa began.

Eyra kept walking toward them. He and Dzifa took a couple more steps back.

The person behind them pressed farther back against the wall. It had to be Marko! Ato remembered Marko's sharp knife slicing smoothly through thick vegetables. Leslie had been right. They never should have come here. His body prickled with panic. The skin across his skull tightened. His breath was escaping in hissy sounds.

He turned around. "Who are y—" he began.

The person clapped a thick hand over Ato's mouth. It was a man's hand.

Ato yanked violently at the hand, trying to get it off his mouth. The hand slid down a fraction and Ato sank his teeth hard into the webbed skin between the man's thumb and forefinger. With a grunt of pain, the man tossed him off.

Still Eyra stood emotionless, just staring at them. Grabbing Dzifa's hand, Ato rocketed past Eyra, toward the garden steps.

"Shoo!" Eyra's voice echoed after them. "Shoo!"

Ato flew down the steps in fright, still holding on to Dzifa. He careered into Leslie and Hafsat, who were huddled behind the bush. From Eyra's garden came a yell and the sound of a door being flung open. Someone appeared from the direction of Marko's cabin. Ato was not going to wait to find out who it was. He and the not-so-Gallant Geese ran all the way down the main path, tripping and stumbling, until they arrived at the foot of Ato's tree cabin.

They collapsed onto the damp, leafy ground, terrified and breathless. Ato inhaled deeply, filling his aching lungs with the sweet woody air.

"My camera," Dzifa panted. "I dropped it. Somewhere. On the way back. I tripped."

Ato clapped his hand to his damp forehead. "Oh no!" His eyes flicked around. Flock Eleven was already stirring to life and a few kids were already down from their cabins, journaling at the bottom of their trees. Several inquisitive eyes were trained on them.

"We'll find your camera later," he said, flicking sweat off his face. "If anyone asks, let's just say we went for a morning run."

Ato recalled with horror the sensation of his teeth against the person's skin, and listened to his teammates' opinions on who the person in the garden could have been. An escaped convict or a mass murderer, Leslie thought. Perhaps someone on the island playing a joke, or someone who wanted to surprise Eyra, possibly a lost relative of hers, Hafsat suggested weakly.

They gave up trying to understand why a person was skulking in Eyra's garden and tried instead to figure out why Eyra had acted so weirdly.

"Why did she look at us so strangely?" Dzifa said, sounding uncharacteristically unnerved.

Ato frowned. "Like she'd never seen us before."

"They told us Eyra was busy," Hafsat said. "Maybe she got so busy that she got tired and forgot who you were."

Ato shook his head. "I know what busy looks like. Sometimes

my mum has lots of people coming to buy fabric in her shop. She gets really tired when the day is over, but she still remembers who I am."

Dzifa agreed. "My mum gets busy drawing all her sketches for houses. But even when she's been up all night, she knows who I am."

"And when my mum is busy—" Leslie began.

"Leslie, your mum's kind is called being a busybody," Dzifa said.

Leslie squared his shoulders to defend his mother. "Do you know what my mum says about your mum?"

"No, we don't know, and let's stop this. This isn't about our mums," Ato cut in.

Hafsat spoke again, thoughtfully. "Maybe Eyra's sick."

Three questioning pairs of eyes turned to her.

"She didn't look sick to me," Ato said.

"Sometimes people can look okay on the outside," she explained. "But if the sickness is mental . . ."

"You're right," Dzifa said slowly.

More and more kids were clambering down from their cabins and getting ready for breakfast. The Gallant Geese scuttled up to their cabins to freshen up. A short while afterward, they were at their table in the Pecking Bowl.

"So we know Eyra won't be in this morning either," Dzifa said, raising a forkful of sweet bambara bean sauce to her lips.

Around the Pecking Bowl, disappointment reflected in the eyes of the kids of Flock Eleven; they had realized Eyra was not going to show up. The Guardians did their best to keep up the cheery atmosphere, singing and clapping and doing a vigorous dance. It drew watery enthusiasm from the children. Everyone wanted to see Eyra.

Ato rested his chin on his hand, poking at his melon-seed bun. "If she's sick, don't we have to tell someone?"

The morning's events had made Leslie hungry. He had taken a generous serving of tamarind-and-pumpkin scones. "Maybe we should just mind our business and stick to our activities," he mumbled through a mouthful of scone.

"Eyra is our friend, Leslie, and if there's something wrong with her we should tell someone," Dzifa replied.

Leslie took another bite of his scone. "Maybe, Dzifa, but then people will know we were snooping about."

Dzifa paused and stirred her forest-fruit smoothie. "I see the kind of friend you are, Leslie. If I were sick, you'd just leave me to die instead of getting me help."

"I wouldn't need to. Ato would tell his nana, and she'd know some plant that would make you better. I bet if she was here she'd put Eyra's head into a pot of boiling leaves like she did with Ato," Leslie said.

"She didn't put my head in the water. Just over the *steam* from the water."

"Cooked your brains properly. That's why you keep doing dangerous stuff," Leslie retorted.

Hafsat sat up straight and held Ato's wrist. "Ato. Maybe you should tell your grandmother about Eyra."

He looked at her thoughtfully. "Maybe I should," he said slowly. But that would have to be after Mission Seven.

CHAPTER TWENTY

TWO HOURS LATER THE GALLANT GEESE STOOD WITH FLOCK Eleven at the foot of the Dawn Locus, in a clearing in the woods. The craggy peak loomed imposingly above them. In some steep spots, steps had been carved into the rock, with rails driven in to aid weary climbers. Through the leafy branches of trees at the foot of the peak, Ato could see falcons perched high up atop the Dawn Locus. They looked like dots from where he stood.

It was a warm Sunday, with barely a cloud in the sky, but this was not why Ato's palms were sweaty. His breathing was rapid and his mouth was dry with anticipation. Eyra had not been able to help him. If he was going to find the plan, the time was now. The plan was up there somewhere. At first he'd thought it might be on the lower grounds, but it was clear that the only place it could be was at the top—where the falcons were. His best bet was to get up there fast, before the Guardians rounded them up and kept them together for the picnic. That meant he couldn't climb up with his team. Climbing up with Leslie and Hafsat would be like trying to walk with school desks chained to each ankle. He would have to move like a falcon. Swiftly. Alone.

"Gather around," Kai called, beckoning them over. Her shoulder muscles bulged beneath her T-shirt. They gathered around her like a flock of blue-and-green birds. Their shoes crunched on the leaves that blanketed the ground, and lizards scuttled away through the undergrowth. Above them glossy fork-tailed drongos, black with glittering red eyes, shrieked out their metallic alarm calls.

Kai checked that shoes were laced and everyone had a water bottle. "Stay with your team," she ordered. "And help each other to the top." She sounded drained and tired.

Ato looked around. Still no sign of Eyra.

Richie came up, wearing hiking gloves and boots that matched his Nnoma T-shirt. He laid out hiking poles in pairs of green, red, blue, and yellow.

"It's gonna be a long walk," he said to them. "You'll need your energy to get to the top. My advice? Be sensible. Climbing to the Dawn Locus is a marathon, not a sprint, so don't slam into it. When you're tired, slow down. Sit if you like. Keep the peak in sight, but don't glue your eyeballs to it so tightly that you don't enjoy the view going up. Get yourself up one step at a time, and before you know it, you'll be waving from the top!"

Kai took Richie's flask from his hand. Leslie made a face.

"One more thing," she cautioned, taking a swig of water. "While going up, keep your steps short and even, and don't raise your knees too high. If you do, you'll tire out in no time. Keep your heart rate steady. Don't overdo it."

Knees and hearts were for old people to worry about, Ato thought scornfully.

Richie picked up two poles and waved them. "You'll find these helpful. This is what you do," he said, placing a pole slightly in front and to the side of his foot before taking a step. "You can't run with them, but they help you heave yourself up."

Ato's father's words re-echoed in his head:

When your steps are strong enough to match mine, we shall walk this mountainside together, to protect this dream.

His dad had definitely not needed a pair of sticks; otherwise, he would have written, *We shall walk this mountainside with sticks.*

Dzifa picked up a pair, as did Hafsat. Leslie picked up three pairs and tried them all out, testing his weight on each one. Ato left his poles on the ground. If he couldn't run with them, they were useless to him.

"No poles, Ato?" Richie looked surprised. "They take the weight off your legs. Plus you've got your backpack with your picnic lunch in it."

"I'll be okay," Ato muttered.

This was going to be the kind of do-or-die moment he had seen in movies, Ato thought. When the hero had to choose between a dangerous move or bitter regret. He had only three days left on Nnoma. Eyra had let him down. This morning there would be no teamwork. It was Ato, the mountain, and the plan. At first everyone would be mad at him for making his crazy move, but when he came out a winner, with the plan to save Nnoma, they'd be slapping him on the back. He still didn't know what

Nnoma's secret was or who Nnoma's enemies were, but maybe the plan would reveal that. He could hear their voices already, congratulating him—his friends, Nana, Mum, Eyra . . .

Closing his eyes to shut out the sight of Flock Eleven kids milling everywhere, he allowed a picture to form in his mind, of himself at the Dawn Locus, waving the plan aloft. A thrill coursed through him. He opened his eyes, smiled, and glugged down some water from his flask. Then he set it by a nearby bush while he re-tied his laces. This was no time to trip. This was time to fly, as fast as a falcon.

CHAPTER TWENTY-ONE

ATO TOOK OFF AT ONCE, STREAKING UP THE MOUNTAINSIDE like a bullet. In no time he would be at the top.

One day, your toes will be firm enough to grip this rock.

He was the son of Ekow Turkson, the man who had helped people believe they could do more than they realized. His father was right—his toes were firm. And his steps were strong! He definitely hadn't needed a stick; there were lots of bushes and branches he could pull himself up by. The rest of Flock Eleven was behind him and he was flying up the mountain like the champion that he was.

His speed increased up the slope. The ground was a blur beneath his strong, swift steps. A breeze behind him seemed to push him along. He smiled. Maybe his father was helping him along.

"Hey, Ato!" a voice called faintly from behind him.

It sounded like Richie. He did not turn around.

"Ato!"

He barreled ahead, pretending not to have heard. He'd

climbed every tree in his home neighborhood and in Turo near his home. The same legs that had taken him up those trees would get him to the Dawn Locus. Short and even steps, Kai had said. Well, how about long and even? Steady rhythm, he told himself. He was breathing in rapid bursts but he was not out of breath. He was Ekow Turkson's son.

His body was warming up. Another thrill surged through him. Intense, they'd said? This was fun! He heard voices behind him. He refused to look back. He knew they wanted him to slow down. They wanted him to be one of the pack. This climb didn't mean anything to them, but it was everything to him. They hadn't had a father who'd helped build Nnoma and who'd left an important plan that would save it from enemies. He kept running—long, fast strides that swallowed up the steep mountainside.

He imagined that to the kids behind him he looked like an arrow streaking up the mountain. The voices behind him receded. Parts of the slope were covered in dead leaves; a couple of times he slipped on them, almost falling, but he steadied himself and kept moving. The sunrays found him through the tree cover and heated his skin. He heard his name called out faintly behind him. He ignored the shouts and kept his pace fast, his steps long. The ground was a brown and green blur beneath his feet. It felt good.

His heart was pounding hard in his chest. He knew he'd be all right. He had his father in him. He looked up. There it was. The Dawn Locus—his goal. It swam in his vision. He blinked hard and kept running. His breathing felt tighter and his throat was dry. He needed a drink. He reached for his flask while he was still in motion. His heart flipped. There was no strap, no flask. He remembered setting it by a bush while he tied his laces. Suddenly his mouth felt sandy and parched. To take his mind off his thirst, he recited the words of his father's letter in his head.

When your steps are strong enough to match mine, we shall walk this mountainside together, to protect this dream . . . You'll prove yourself good enough to come here.

He was doing even better than his dad had hoped, he thought: he was flying up the mountain! The advice from the Guardians echoed in his head.

When you're tired, slow down.

Today's climb is a marathon, not a sprint,

Don't slam into it.

He gritted his teeth. He would not stop. He would not slow down. Not when the plan was waiting at the top. The trees had given way to shorter shrubs and the sun was an unobstructed orb of yellow lava in the sky. Sweat streamed from his forehead, trickling into his eyes, along his nose, and dripping from his chin. Invisible flames licked at his calves. He glanced back. Everyone else was far behind. But someone was coming close—Richie. He had to move faster. If Richie caught up with him, he would stop him from searching around the falcons. The flames in his calves leapt up into his arms and his chest. His lungs were on fire. His eyes felt like hot marbles in their sockets. The peak was close, so close. But there was something wrong—his breath wasn't getting all the way down. A force was squeezing his windpipe shut and his breath was a rattling whistle. His skin was burning. But several painful strides later, he was at the top. The island of Nnoma lay spread out beneath him in a confusing haze of green, brown, and blue. But he didn't want the view of Nnoma. He wanted something else. He glanced around wildly, sweat stinging his eyes. There they were—the rocks. Several falcons were perched on its craggy ledges overlooking the valley.

I have a plan. It is protected, somewhere below this rock peak, where the sunlight first greets Nnoma, where the falcons watch over the valley.

He ran toward the falcons—his friends. They had protected the plan. Now he was on the rocks, clambering up toward the ledge of the Dawn Locus. He looked down and saw the drop of a few hundred feet. His stomach churned and he drew back, shaken. But it had to be here, he told himself. He would find it.

A blur of white and gray flashed in front of him. Falcons. Two of them. No, three. Four. They were diving toward him. He knew what falcons were like—they would attack anything that strayed into their territory. But these were his friends. A sharp, curved beak was heading straight for his eyes. He saw a flash of yellow, hooked talons, outstretched.

Instantly he realized: he was an enemy.

The falcons circled above him, golden eyes glittering with hostile intent. He knew they would usually only attack him if his back was turned. He had to face them. But he was frightened. His eyes! They would gouge them out and eat them like a vulture would! So he flung himself facedown on the ground.

A blow glanced across his shoulder. The whoosh of air from

a powerful set of wings. Talons raking along his backpack. The tug of his T-shirt snagged by something sharp. A ripping sound. He covered the back of his head with his hands. His heart crashed wildly within his chest. There were two more blows to his shoulders and his neck. He was afraid to move. Then he heard a voice from a distance.

He heard frantic shouts. People were close by. He scrambled to his feet and tried to run, but a savage cramp seized his calves. He doubled over. His muscles kept tightening; an excruciating pain shot from his legs into his stomach and his arms. His fingers curled in agony. The world circled around him in slow motion. People were coming. Their outlines were blurry, so blurry. They looked like vultures, gathering around him. Then the ground was rushing up to meet him.

CHAPTER TWENTY-TWO

AN HOUR LATER, ATO LAY FACING THE WINDOW IN THE Healing Cabin, brooding over his disgrace. Creamy calico curtains shielded him from the glare of the outside sun. The room was cool and quiet, and there was no one else save Richie and Bea. Bea fussed over him with a thermometer, antiseptic lotion for his grazes, and a cool facecloth on his forehead.

He kept his eyes closed. He had no desire to see anyone. He remembered his legs giving way, the dull thud of his head hitting the ground. He remembered the feeling of helplessness. Why had his father put the plan so far out of reach if he had wanted him to find it? Back home, Leslie had said the plan had probably been eaten by rats. Maybe he was right.

"Ato."

He reluctantly cracked an eye open. Richie was staring down at him with an inscrutable look on his face.

"Feeling better? Do you want to tell me what that was all about?"

No, he didn't want to talk to Richie. Or to anyone else. So

much for flying up the mountain. Now he just wanted the wings of a falcon so he could fly off home. Or the wings of a goose. Any old bird wings would do, in fact. He pressed his cheek into the crisp cotton of his pillow, the ache of despair spreading through him. "I'm sorry." His tongue was stuck to the roof of his mouth and his words came out as a raspy lisp.

"You're sorry? You take off like a jackrabbit, at ridiculous speed. You leave your team and everyone else behind. I have to chase you *all the way up*. Then you run over to the falcons, the *wild* falcons, and dangle yourself over a dangerous ledge? What were you thinking?" Richie's face reflected concern . . . and anger.

Ato was silent. His lips were glued together by shame.

Richie turned away. "I'll be back," he said.

Ato could tell Richie was holding back from giving him a full telling-off. No doubt that would come as soon as he was out of the Healing Cabin, he thought gloomily.

After Richie had left, Bea offered him a few sips of cool coconut water, and touched his forehead again. She seemed satisfied, and with a final tug to draw his curtains closer together, she left the room. Ato turned his face to the wall. He would never live down the humiliation of being carried down the mountain by Richie, his head lolling about like a rag doll's. He had protested, and tried to walk, but Richie would have none of it.

"Sorry, kid. I have zero trust for you on these slopes," Richie had said, and with that, he had hoisted him onto his broad back like a sack of corn. Shame seared through Ato, as he remembered the looks from everyone, some pitying, many amused. Bello's scornful look. He would never forget this day. Neither would anyone else, he was sure. He blinked back the hot sting of tears.

When your steps are strong enough to match mine, we shall walk this mountainside together. That hadn't happened. His legs had melted to jelly. The falcons had turned against him. He'd become so used to seeing the painting of a peregrine falcon in his room at Nana's that he'd thought of falcons as being his friends, watching over him. He'd spoken to the one on his ceiling so many times, lying on his back at night while it kept an eye on him. He felt partly betrayed, but mostly angry with himself for his foolishness. Richie was right—they were wild animals.

Bea came in with some more coconut water, which he drank gratefully. She tiptoed away and he closed his eyes. The door swung open yet again and he heard whispering by his bedside. His eyes flickered open and he turned to see Leslie and Dzifa standing beside his bed. Hafsat stood farther behind, hands clasped, watching him with sympathetic eyes.

"He's awake," Dzifa declared triumphantly. She bent over him. "Dumbo! You chose the hottest morning so far to fly up the mountain. Did you think you were a bird? Richie had to scrape your passed-out body off the ground. We thought you were a goner!"

"Lactic acid," Leslie said. "Bello said something about that. He said you ran so fast that it built up in your muscles and then they got painful and stopped working."

Trust Leslie to think he'd care for a biology lesson from Profess-O Bello now, Ato thought morosely.

It sounded as if climbing the peak had been a challenge for a number of teams. Not everybody finished, Leslie told him cheerfully. A number of kids totally panicked at the steepness of the climb and turned back. Several others were too tired and too hot to make it to the top.

"*We* got to the top. But we missed the picnic because of you," Leslie added. "We came back down to see you."

"You should have stayed," he mumbled through stiff lips.

"We're teammates," Leslie said righteously. "We wanted to make sure you weren't dying. This team stays together."

His friends had come down with him. They hadn't stayed until the end of the picnic. Maybe that was supposed to make him feel better, but it didn't. He just felt another wash of shame. Once again he hoped they would vanish. Or that he would.

Dzifa sat on the edge of his bed and lowered her face until her forehead was almost touching his. "You ran up to find the plan, didn't you?"

He nodded feebly. Dzifa and Leslie sighed in unison.

"I thought it would be up there. *Where the falcons watch over the valley*," he whispered.

"You're lucky loads of other kids didn't finish the climb. I would have killed you," Dzifa remarked. "We're in fourth place—just two points behind the Falcons. But we've got to give Mission Eight our *everything*."

"Would your dad put the plan in such a dangerous place?" Leslie asked, giving Ato a look that made him feel foolish.

"I don't think your dad would have wanted to disturb the

falcons. It's probably in a place that animals would stay *away* from," Hafsat said.

Leslie wagged a lecturing finger. "Do you think your dad would have been impressed if you'd died at the top and the vultures had picked your eyes out, then your tongue, and then the rest of you?"

"Stop it, Leslie," Hafsat chided.

For the second time, Ato felt the sting of tears. Maybe he was a fool. A proper goose.

Kai strode in and shooed his friends out. A while after that, Frank the Tank brought in a tray of food for Ato, a late lunch. He picked at the food and then pushed the tray away. His mind turned to Eyra. When Richie walked in several long minutes later, his mind was still on her.

"Is there anything wrong with Eyra, Richie?" he burst out.

Richie clasped his hands behind his back and studied him the way a headmaster would inspect a wayward student. "I was coming back to ask what was wrong with *you*," he said calmly, his previous anger clearly having subsided. "But what makes you ask about Eyra?"

"I just, umm . . . just wondered?"

"Same way the Guardians wondered whose camera was left in the bushes a few feet from Eyra's garden this morning?"

Ato bit his lip.

Richie gave him a long, searching look. When he spoke, his voice was low and firm.

"Listen, Ato. Eyra spends all her time and energy planning

for you guys to come here, so she needs some quiet time. Time to think and plan great things for the Asafo and for Nnoma. Imagine what would happen if every kid here went crawling around her and her cabin like lice. She would be exhausted. And now in particular Eyra has been very busy, talking to important people who are interested in Nnoma. Nnoma is well known around the globe, you see." His tone softened. "Don't worry. She'll make it up to you."

Ato felt Richie's words crush his heart. *Lice.* He squeezed his eyes shut to blink back tears. Eyra *had* said they could come to her cabin. Had she changed her mind? With only about two days to go?

When he opened his eyes, Richie was still watching him.

Richie stepped away. "Get some rest, Ato. I'll see you later."

Suddenly every dream he'd had before coming to Nnoma crumbled away. Even Eyra didn't seem to care much for them anymore. He missed home. And Mum. And especially Nana—he wanted to talk to her more than anyone else in the world.

CHAPTER TWENTY-THREE

ATO REACHED OUT FROM HIS BED, PUSHED BACK THE curtain, and looked out the window. Outside, kids played in the stream. Golden flecks of sunshine reflected off the rippling water. Their laughter mingled with the cries of island birds. Watching them from the Healing Cabin, he felt far away from it all, as if he were watching them from a distant planet. The door swung open and a head poked through: Hafsat.

"Hey." Her eyes wavered with uncertainty.

He wasn't happy to see her. He wanted to be alone on his planet. She walked in anyway.

"What are you doing up here? Everyone is down there. Having fun."

She shrugged. "I told them I had a tummy ache. I wanted to see you." Her brown eyes held his. "Sorry about today."

"I don't want to talk about it," he muttered, looking down. He hoped she would go away soon.

"I know how that feels. Not wanting to talk about things."

There was a long silence, broken by the on-and-off scream of a bird outside. Probably a black-and-white plover, he thought.

He turned back to Hafsat. She had sat on the floor cross-legged, twisting and untwisting her fingers.

"I'm sorry I spoke about your dad," he mumbled.

"I don't like talking about what happened to my dad." She didn't sound mad. She sounded sad. It made him feel even worse. And he already felt terrible after the day he'd had. Her next words cheered him up.

"You're a good friend, Ato," she continued. "You were still kind to me even when I didn't tell you the truth about my dad." She clasped her hands tightly together, looking out the window with unseeing eyes. "It was so sudden, the way they took Daddy," she said. "Not that long before we came to Nnoma. We were coming back from my cousin's birthday party. She's twelve, like me. Dad had bought her a drone and everyone had given it a try. He always gives . . . gave cool presents. And we—my mum, my dad, my brother, and me—we were talking about how much fun it was. We pushed our front gate open. That's when they came in. Behind us."

"Who?"

"Police." She shook her head as if trying to shake the image away. Her eyes were fixed on the sunny outdoors beyond the window. "It felt like there were a thousand of them. Later on Mum said there were seven. They were everywhere." Her eyes brightened with tears. "I thought they'd come to the wrong house.

Daddy was speaking to them in a low voice. 'Not in front of my family,' he kept begging. I guess he knew why they'd come." She brushed the back of her hand across her eyes.

"Then what happened?" he asked, despite himself. He could see it hurt her to talk about it.

"They . . ." She touched her wrists together.

He got it. Handcuffs.

"Mum said they'd got the wrong man. She ran after them and was holding on to my dad's shirt. She even ran ahead and padlocked the gate, but they just smashed it. Dad told her everything would be okay. But everything wasn't okay. They took him away. And I ran and hid. I was scared. I thought they were going to take me away too."

A well of sympathy rose inside Ato. He did not know what to say to her, but he didn't need to say anything just yet. Hafsat had more to say.

"Every night I had nightmares. I was afraid the police were going to come and take my mum away. When the doorbell rang, I'd be so scared that sometimes I'd throw up. When a door slammed, Mum would jump as if a gun had gone off." She wrung her hands. "My dad was going to prison, for a long time. 'Cos, he'd taken money from where he worked. A lot. And then it was on the news—Sunshine TV."

Sunshine TV! It dawned on Ato that this was probably why Hafsat had looked uncomfortable when Dzifa had first mentioned the station. Did Max know anything about Hafsat's father? he wondered. Maybe he'd even broken the news about him—after all, Max was the main crime reporter for Sunshine TV.

"So at school everyone started giving me funny looks. Kids would be talking, but when I got there, they would stop. I just wanted to leave, to go far away, where nobody knew us." A sad smile formed on her lips. "We moved. We couldn't stay in our house anymore—Mum couldn't afford it. And I didn't want to go to school anymore, 'cos kids were being mean. Mum started homeschooling me. When I came here, I wanted to pretend nothing had ever happened."

"I'm so sorry," Ato said softly.

A lonely tear trickled past her nose. "Mum won't take me to the prison. She doesn't call him or visit him. She doesn't talk about him. She's mad at him. It really feels like he's . . . dead." She licked the tear and sniffed. "I miss him."

"Of course you do," Ato said gently. "You'll get to see him again one day, Hafsat, but it's understandable to miss him."

"I thought it was my fault. That maybe my dad took the money so he could buy stuff to make me happy. Richie told me it wasn't my fault."

"He knows about your dad?"

She nodded. "He's even met him. At the prison. Richie had gone to see someone else. Richie makes me feel better."

She played with her fingers for several minutes. Then she looked straight at him.

"Ato, people might think you're stupid for running up the mountain like that today. But I don't. I think you're brave. I want to be brave too. I've been thinking a lot about what Eyra told me at our dinner that evening. She told me to face hard situations, and that I am stronger than I think I am." She exhaled and stood up. "I'm going to the Chirp and Chatter right now. I know where my dad's prison is—Nsawam. I'll ask Clara to help me phone him." She looked straight at him. "And I've been afraid to ask my mum this, but when I go home I'm going to tell her that I have to see him. I know he did something wrong; but . . . he's still my dad."

She left the room, quietly closing the door behind her.

For the first time that afternoon, Ato smiled. "Gallant," he said to himself.

♦ ♦ ♦ ♦ ♦ ♦ ♦

A few hours later, Ato was hobbling out of the Healing Cabin. A Guardian had brought him an early dinner and watched him carefully while he ate. Satisfied that apart from muscle soreness and his superficial scratches he was all right, she had allowed him out. He went straight to the Chirp and Chatter, where Clara was watching a monkey juggling water bottles on the big screen.

Yes, of course he could make a phone call, she said with a compassionate nod, handing him a phone.

"Hafsat was here too," Clara added, dropping her voice. "She was on the phone for a long time."

Ato wondered what Clara had heard, but he didn't like to ask. Would Hafsat tell him about her chat with her dad? he wondered. He promised himself not to pry. If she wanted to tell him, she would.

"Nana!" he exclaimed when his grandmother answered. Her warm voice flooded him with comfort.

"My darling! Are you having a wonderful time?"

He sighed. "Not really, Nana."

"Do you want to tell me about it?"

He did. Slumping down with his back against the wall and his aching legs stretching out into the corridor, he told Nana about everything: from not finding the plan to Eyra who was not meeting for meals anymore, her strange behavior that morning, to his disastrous run up the Dawn Locus.

Nana listened closely, soothing him with calming and encouraging words. When he was done, she fell silent.

"Are you there, Nana?" he asked.

"I am. Eyra is on my mind." She sounded oddly worried. "This strange behavior you describe from this morning, it reminds me of something."

"What, Nana?" There was something odd about her voice.

She let out a long breath. "Ato, maybe I've seen and heard too much, but I'm concerned about her behavior. Suddenly speaking strangely. Acting odd. Not recognizing you. It makes me wonder . . ."

"Wonder what, Nana?"

"It makes me wonder what she's been eating. Or drinking."

Ato frowned. "She only eats natural things—flowers and grains and roots and weeds. Stuff like that."

There was a pause. "I see," Nana said thoughtfully. "That isn't always a good thing. Not all natural things are meant to be eaten."

Where had he heard that before?

"Now listen to me, Ato. Today you need to rest. But

tomorrow, and I hope that won't be too late, I want you to look out for something. Ask your friends to help you, but don't tell anyone else. No one. Phone me and tell me if you found it."

"But if what you want me to look for is so important, why can't we tell anyone else?"

"Because if the wrong person knows you're looking for it, it might put you in danger."

CHAPTER TWENTY-FOUR

HEART POUNDING, ATO SHUFFLED OUT OF THE CHIRP AND Chatter into the cool evening air. Nana never made a big deal about anything. Unlike his mum, who had once made a fuss for three days because his teacher had told her he was making paper ostriches during class instead of paying attention. But this time it sounded like a big deal. That troubled him. Maybe if Nana were here he would feel braver, especially since somewhere out there a scary man was probably still skulking around. He shivered.

Kids were leaving the Pecking Bowl in straggly groups and heading to their cabins for an early night. He overheard their remarks—many of them were unhappy about Eyra's no-show for dinner. Several kids passed sympathetic comments when they saw him. A few cheered his mountain run. Bello sneered about a wild goose chase. Ato pretended to smile; he'd brought it on himself, after all. When he saw his teammates, he waved them over to him. Avoiding their questions about how he felt, he dived straight into his phone call with his grandmother and what she had asked him to do.

Dzifa cocked her head, puzzled. "Eyra is acting weird and your Nana wants us to look for flowers that look like *trumpets*?"

He nodded. "Trumpets turned upside down. They can be white, yellow, or even purple."

Leslie looked equally bemused. "A trumpet turned upside down," he repeated.

"That's what she said. She wouldn't ask us to look if it wasn't important."

"I've seen them," Hafsat said slowly. She had a funny look on her face, as if she were forcing a picture into her mind.

Ato grabbed her hand. "Where?"

"Umm . . . umm . . ." Her face fell. "I can't remember."

Dzifa blew out a breath impatiently. "Hafsat, are you sure you even saw it?"

"I . . . I think so . . ." But her voice was unconvincing.

At that moment, familiar lilting chimes filled the air. Bedtime.

"Maybe tomorrow you'll remember?" Ato said to Hafsat, trying to make her feel better.

She nodded. "Maybe."

They headed up together toward their cabins. Ato struggled to keep up with them: every movement sent pain radiating through his legs. "Let's see if we can all search for the flower tomorrow morning," he said, wincing.

"D'you think we should?" Leslie chewed his lip, doubt heavy in his voice. "Your nana said it might put us in danger. And maybe we're overthinking this Eyra business. Richie said she was busy."

"That's what he *said*."

Hafsat stopped. "Are you saying he's lying?"

"I dunno." Ato spread out his arms as far as his aching shoulders would allow. "Did she look busy to you?" A knot was forming in his stomach. With only two days to go, this Nnoma trip was heading in a weird direction.

"By the way, something's definitely up with Kai," Dzifa said as they approached their cabins. "She looks super-stressed-out now. And she's always looking around as if she's expecting some giant hawk to snatch up one of us . . . or her. Anyways." She yawned. "It's good night from me."

Ato dreamt about flowers all night. Huge yellow-and-white flowers with legs and arms. They marched down the street, blowing trumpets at a deafening volume while he chased them, trying in vain to catch them.

"We *are* going to look for the flower today, aren't we?" he asked his team at breakfast the next morning.

Dzifa was munching on a wild-berry-and-barley cake. She paused mid-chew. "Yah. Also, you do know this is our last mission. And we're two points behind third place?"

Leslie pretended not to have heard Ato, bending over his bowl of food and chomping with great concentration. Hafsat played with her food, breaking off her fonio-and-banana muffins and scattering the crumbs about her plate.

It would be wonderful if they found the plan while they were looking for the flower, Ato thought for one wistful, fleeting moment. But they had only two days to go on Nnoma. With no Eyra, it would be a miracle if he found it.

An hour later, the Gallant Geese embarked on Home in Harmony with Nature, the eighth and final mission: to build a mini-model human home from natural materials. The wider the variety of natural materials, and the stronger their model, the higher their score. Having more creatures around their model also meant more points. Any wildlife found in or around the mini-building would attract more points. Mission Eight was a long one—three hours in the morning, and another two hours after Nest Rest.

That morning Ato kept his eyes open for the trumpet-shaped flower as he and his team gathered bamboo, grass, earth, wood, and stone for their mini-home. Choosing a spot took some time, but eventually they settled on a spot close to the stream that trickled into the lake.

While they pressed bricks of straw and mud, his limbs felt even more sore than they had the day before. Press on gallantly, Ato, he thought, grimacing. They coaxed several giant snails near to their project, along with a green and yellow spider the size of a small saucer.

As Leslie laid homemade bricks on top of each other, he stumbled onto a four-foot monitor lizard.

"Aargh," he screamed at the sight of its flicking, forked blue tongue. Ato could not convince him that the lizard did not consider him part of the food chain. For the rest of the morning Leslie kept one hand curled around the pepper spray he had hidden in his pocket.

By lunchtime, the Gallant Geese were pleased with their efforts.

"This is great," Hafsat said proudly. "After lunch we can choose the shrubs and flowers to put around our home to bring in the bees and bugs and butterflies . . . and birds."

"My grandmother's garden is like that," Ato said proudly. "Full of all kinds of creatures." He decided it was not necessary to mention that his mother had paved over their tiny patch of garden with concrete slabs.

Beside him, Hafsat stiffened. He gave her a questioning glance.

"Ato!" Hafsat exclaimed. "Eyra's garden—that's where I saw the flower!"

CHAPTER TWENTY-FIVE

IMMEDIATELY AFTER LUNCH, INSTEAD OF HEADING TO THEIR cabins for Nest Rest, the Gallant Geese disappeared through the dense undergrowth that led from their cabins to Eyra's. They wore green Nnoma T-shirts to blend in as best as they could with their background. Ato's mind had been so consumed by thoughts of the plan that he hadn't given much thought to the mysterious man in Eyra's garden, but now a pang of worry jolted through his stomach. He hoped he wouldn't have to bite his way out like last time. This time the sunshine was a bright and comforting contrast from the gloom of their dawn visit.

"We just want to see if the flower is there," Ato said.

Leslie brushed a cobweb off his face. "That plus the mass murderer who's waiting to kill us all."

Ato sighed testily. "Leslie, if that person had wanted to kill us I'm sure he could have. You would have been an easy catch. We just need to find out if Hafsat is right so we can tell Nana," he said with a nonchalance he did not feel, secretly thinking Leslie might be right. He pushed the thought away. No time for that now, there was a mission to complete.

They got to Eyra's part of the island with no trouble. The bigger trouble, Ato realized, as they skulked in the thick brush that grew around her cabin, was how to get up the steps into Eyra's garden without being noticed.

"This way," Ato whispered, pointing back the way they had come. Crouching low, almost on all fours, he led them through the thick foliage around the back of the cabin all the way to the bramble-covered slope that rose up to meet the far end of the bottom of Eyra's garden. Hafsat looked up at the rough stones and prickly bushes. Her eyes widened in consternation.

Gritting his teeth, Ato took the lead. He grasped a stone and heaved himself up the hostile incline. He soon realized the climb was not as hard as it looked. Ignoring a few pricks from the thorny brambles, and blocking out Leslie's warnings about tetanus and lockjaw, he made it to the top. To his relief, so did everyone else.

Once in the garden, he scuttled ahead with the others trailing him. He paused behind a bush and peered around. Apart from the shrilling treetop birds, the garden was deserted.

"There," Hafsat whispered from behind him.

Three pairs of eyes followed the direction of Hafsat's finger. Behind the tree where they had sat to dine with Eyra, hidden by a tangle of shrubs and wildflowers, were purple flowers. Trumpet-shaped. And dangling downward.

Ato suddenly lost feeling in his legs. Nana's words rang

through his head: *If the wrong person knows you're looking for it, it might put you in danger.*

Behind him Dzifa inhaled sharply as Marko appeared from inside the cabin. In his hand was his steel knife, flashing in the sunlight. He stood for a moment, still as a pencil, his head turning slowly as if he were looking from one end of the garden to the other. He tilted his head back, as though he were sniffing the air. Ato held his breath, terrified of making a sound. The fear from their last trip here came rushing back. Had Marko been the person skulking in the shadows that morning? But if so, who had come running out of Marko's bungalow?

He watched in trepidation as the cook moved with ease to a tap sticking out of the ground, wet the blade, and sharpened it on a round rock on the ground.

Ato's stomach tightened at the whine of hard metal on stone. A memory flashed into his head of going with his mother to the market to buy a chicken. With one thick hand, the butcher had grasped the live chicken's head and pinned down its wings. Ato remembered the swift flick of the butcher's wrist. The chicken had jerked, flapped, spurted blood, and died, all while being held down.

The butcher had glanced at his anguished face. "Don't you eat chicken?" he had sneered. Ato's face and ears had felt hot. He liked chicken stew. And grilled chicken. But he didn't want to know how it got to his plate.

Ato's heart stopped. Marko had raised his head, facing in their direction. In a move faster than Ato could have thought possible,

Marko darted across the garden, dived into the bushes, and grabbed Ato's wrist.

Ato screamed in terror. Marko's knife brought back a horrifying vision of the chicken's dark red blood.

"Let him go!" Dzifa yelled, grasping Marko's throat in her small hands.

With a choking cry, Leslie sprang out of the bushes, followed closely by Hafsat. From the corner of his eye, Ato saw them flee down the stony incline and disappear.

"Shhh!" Marko held the knife to his lips and shook Dzifa off like a fly. She tumbled backward and sprang to her feet. Ato was held in a bear grip. The knife was a couple of inches from his face. But the cook did not seem interested in using the knife. He dropped it and grabbed Dzifa's wrist.

"Childrens." His voice was low, gruff. "Is it you doing somethings to Madam Eyra?"

"What?" Ato strained to free himself.

"Some peepos is doing something to Eyra."

"I haven't done anything to her."

"I hear you the last time you come here. I smell you. Childrens. Coming here early in the morning."

"We haven't done anything!" Ato protested. He and Dzifa kept trying to wrest themselves away. It was fruitless. Marko had the strength of a gorilla.

Then, just as suddenly as he had grabbed them, Marko's arms went limp. He let go of them and dropped to his knees.

"I dunno what is happening to Madam Eyra." Gone was the

fierce man who had attacked them minutes ago. Now he looked wretched, forlorn. "She not herself. It be like somebody living in her body. Three days now."

Ato felt a stab of sympathy at the despair in Marko's voice.

"And I hear peepos. Near here, when I am making her drink. Eyra do not hear them, but I hear them. Near her table."

Ato was torn between running as far away from the garden as possible and finding out more. His curiosity overcame him.

"What do you think is happening, Marko?"

"I duna know. Madam Eyra is sick. She not herself. She somebody else. And I duna know why." His voice turned harsh. "Go away."

Marko stumbled across the garden into his cabin and Ato hurried off with Dzifa to find their teammates.

Fifteen minutes later Ato hobbled into the Chirp and Chatter. He had left his teammates hiding behind a nearby grove of palm nut trees. Clara looked up in surprise.

"No Nest Rest?"

"I got permission to call my Nana," he lied.

The young woman held on to the phone for several moments, pointing out a copper-tailed starling perching on the window ledge. She seemed to think Ato was interested in how often it visited her. He was not. He snatched the phone from her so fast that he had to apologize. Hurrying out the door, he crouched behind the pile of cushions where he would remain unseen by any Guardian who strayed in. He tapped out Nana's number on the smooth keypad.

Nana answered on the second ring.

"Nana," he whispered, covering his mouth with his hand. "We found it. The flower. It's in Eyra's garden."

There was silence on the other end. But he knew Nana was still there. She was thinking.

Pa-pum-pa-pum-pa-pum. His heart thudded like a talking drum. A frantic talking drum. He knew Nana. She was worried— something was wrong. A lump of anxiety formed in his stomach. He glanced at Clara, hoping she was not looking in his direction. Happily, the bird at her window still held her attention.

"Ato, I want you to stay calm. And to be very careful." Nana sounded calm but grave. "There might be people on Nnoma who'll do anything to have their way. That flower looks beautiful. But it can be used for something that's not so beautiful. When it's put in a drink, it can stop people from thinking their own thoughts."

Ato's own thoughts began whirling in dizzying circles. "You think someone . . . the flower . . . Eyra . . . ?"

"Yes, Ato. I do believe someone may be using that flower on Eyra."

His fingers slackened in shock. Was someone playing a horrible joke on Eyra? Two questions tumbled about in the spin cycle that was his brain: Why was someone giving this flower to Eyra? And who was that someone?

In that second, he remembered the sharp ending to Nana's phone conversation with Max on the day he'd left for Nnoma. The conversation about a secret.

"Nana," he blurted. "There's a secret on Nnoma, isn't there? Are you hiding something from me?"

"Yes." Nana's voice came back without hesitation, firm and quiet. "Yes, Ato, I *am* keeping something from you."

Ato's hand began to shake.

"Nana, what's going on?"

"There's something on Nnoma that people want. Badly enough to destroy the island. Your father knew this. That's why he spoke of a plan to protect Nnoma." She paused. "I hoped with all my heart that his fears would not come true. But I see I hoped in vain."

"What is it, Nana? What is here?" His lips had gone rubbery.

"Ato, knowledge without wisdom is like water in the sand. Whether I tell you or not is not important. Now listen. This is the important thing: Nnoma is in danger. We have two choices. To do something. Or nothing. Which will it be?"

CHAPTER TWENTY-SIX

BACK BEHIND THE GROVE, ATO LOOKED FROM ONE ASTON-
ished face to another.

Dzifa clapped her hands to her face in disbelief. "So that's why
Eyra stopped coming to the Pecking Bowl with us? Someone is
controlling her? By poisoning her brain? Why? Who?"

"I dunno. How insane does that sound? But that's what my
grandmother thinks. And she said if we want to do something,
then we have to move. Fast."

"Yes, away from this killer island. Far away." Leslie's voice
was a strangled squeak. He glanced around quickly. "I bet it's Kai!
Remember how she said we should all die?"

Blood throbbed in Ato's temples.

"So what do we do?" Hafsat asked, shifting from foot to foot
nervously.

Ato's mind flashed to his father. *He had a gift; he encouraged
people to do more than they thought they could.* Those were Eyra's
words. His hands were clammy and his mouth was dry, but he was
his father's son. There was only one thing to do.

"Nana told me what we need to do to stop the flower from working on Eyra's brain. She said we needed to find these." He began counting on trembling fingers. "First, a handful of the tiny red flowers with four petals that grow near waterweeds. Next, guava leaves, four or five of them. Then the root of a creeping plant with thin leaves and flat purple flowers that grows on dry, rocky ground. And last, little yellow flowers from the cassia tree."

"What? It'll take us hours to find all those!" Dismay crept into Dzifa's voice.

"I know." Ato looked at the ground. The rest of his words were left unspoken. But he knew they all understood. They would not be able to finish Mission Eight.

"We're"—Leslie brought his forefinger and thumb a centimeter apart—"*this* close to becoming Asafo."

A lump formed in Ato's throat. His hand crept to his heart. "Would we really be Asafo here . . . inside us . . . if . . . if we just left Eyra?" he asked hesitantly.

There was an aching, throbbing silence. Ato felt the hot prickle of tears. He blinked hard. Dzifa's eyes sparkled too. She brushed the tear away roughly. Hafsat sniffed, and Leslie let out a long sigh.

When Dzifa spoke, her voice was gruff. "And when we find Nana's plants? Then what? What did your grandmother say we had to do?"

"Dzifa," he muttered. He hugged her tightly. Leslie drew up close and wrapped his arms around them. Ato felt Hafsat's arm around his shoulder. The Gallant Geese stood in a huddle, silently mourning the loss of their dream.

Leslie drew away first. "So we won't make the mission. We'll lose our points. It's not the end of the world," he said in a voice that sounded like it was the end of the world.

Dzifa's tone was terse. "Go on, Ato. What do we do?"

"Boil them together for five minutes. Then give Eyra a cupful to drink." He hoped he didn't sound as pessimistic as he felt.

"Did you say *boil*?" Leslie looked aghast. "How are we going to do that?"

"I thought . . . maybe Marko?" Ato's words faltered.

Leslie clapped his hands to his head. "Marko the mass murderer with his knife? He'll boil *us*, that's what he'll do!"

"If he wanted to kill us he could have done that today," Dzifa said.

"We'll worry about Marko later. Right now let's start looking." Ato tried not to think about how difficult it was going to be to search for plants on an island this big.

Dzifa looked toward the cabins. Nest Rest Hour was almost up. "Everyone will be out soon. Let's see if each of us can find something."

"We have to stay together," Leslie protested. "This is what happens in the horror films—everyone goes a different way and then the bad guy catches each person one by one. Plus we don't even know where to start looking!"

Hafsat frowned thoughtfully, unhooked the camera from around her neck, and began to flick rapidly through her pictures, muttering to herself. Ato, Dzifa, and Leslie crowded around her as one by one she went through dozens and dozens of images. They each understood what she was doing. She's a genius, Ato thought admiringly. The tiny red flowers were near the raft bay. The guava tree was at the bottom of Woodside. The little yellow flowers on the far side of the Chirp and Chatter. The creeping plant with flat purple flowers . . . she paused and thought long and hard. She didn't have a picture of that.

She clasped her hands to her mouth, eyes closed, muttering to herself while they watched her, willing her to remember.

Then she opened her eyes. "The cave! Mission Five. I saw them when I went around the cave, when you were picking the bird pictures off the wall!"

The other three looked at her in astonishment. Dzifa looked dumbstruck. "You're the best, Hafsat," she said, when she finally found her voice.

"Let's do this," Hafsat said.

Nearly an hour later, the Gallant Geese set off through the bushes for Eyra's, their plant medicines hidden in their pockets. They had fooled the Guardians, telling them that they were hunting for materials for Mission Eight. Getting the purple flowers had been the hardest part; they were so far away, and rafting was out of the question. But Dzifa had gone to get them. She was the fastest runner, and once she had Hafsat's directions, she had streaked across Rockside to get to the slopes behind the cave. The flowers had been exactly where Hafsat had described them.

To get to Eyra's they had decided to stay off the path. The Guardians would be actively looking for them by now. Ato glanced behind him. Nnoma lay spread out like the centerfold of a nature magazine. Could anything horrible happen in a place as beautiful as this? The voices of children on their last mission carried up to his ears. Pain stabbed at his chest. Mission Eight. They had been so close. Now they would not be Asafo. And he had not found the plan.

He halted abruptly as his friends hurried on ahead.

Could it be? His heart rate picked up, even faster than it already was. A thought had formed clear as daylight. The plan! Had it been closer to him than he could have dreamt? Close enough to touch? Hidden, and yet in the center of everything? Oh, how he wanted to run back now, to look—

"Hey!" Dzifa had turned around with a frown.

He hovered, torn by a powerful urge to run back and hunt out what he had dreamt about for so long.

Leslie had turned around too. A look of relief had appeared on his face. "Oh good. He's changed his mind."

Think too about what would be good for everyone. That's what's best. Because you too are part of "everyone."

Nana's words echoed in his heart. He knew there was only one thing he could do at this moment: put the plan behind him for now and help save Eyra.

"Let's go!" he declared.

And, taking several firm steps, he moved ahead of the Gallant Geese, leading them to Eyra's cabin.

CHAPTER TWENTY-SEVEN

AT EYRA'S CABIN THEY SLUNK UP TO THE STEEP GARDEN STEPS.

"Wait for me," Ato whispered. He gathered their plant medicines in his hands.

"This is a nightmare. One hundred percent," Leslie said in a voice thin with fear.

Ato stole below the cabin windows, which opened out to the garden. Inside, Eyra sat perfectly still on a stool with her back to him. He scuttled along the grounds to Marko's cabin and pushed the door open.

"Who dat?" The cook reached for something on the table. A knife.

Ato gulped. "It's me, Ato."

Marko grabbed his wrist. "One of the childrens. What you wanting?"

"Listen!" Ato dumped the herbs on the table and whispered Nana's instructions urgently, his breath hot in his throat, wondering if he dared hope that Marko would help him.

The cook's hand tightened around his wrist. Ato felt his heart would burst out of his chest. In a lightning move, the cook shoved him into a large cupboard. Ato had no time to react. He gave a small cry of alarm as the latch turned. He was locked in.

"You stay here," Marko growled from the other side of the door.

Terrified, Ato shook the cupboard door. The lock rattled but did not budge. He banged on the door and kicked hard, but it must have been created to withstand a bomb blast. Ato trembled in the warm, stifling space. Why had Marko locked him in? It didn't make sense! He'd told Marko he was here to help Eyra. He thought Marko wanted that too! Didn't Marko believe him?

He considered screaming for help. The thought of Marko attempting to silence him with his knife stopped him. For a panicky moment, he feared he would run out of oxygen. He forced himself to breathe slowly. His heart rate began to slow down. His friends would soon start wondering why he hadn't come out.

He counted up to one hundred. Then two hundred. Five hundred. Eight hundred. At nine hundred and ninety-nine, he clenched his fist to bang on the door again. At that moment, it swung open. He toppled out onto the stone-tiled floor.

Marko sat him up and held a steaming cup to his lips.

"I do it. I will give to Madam Eyra. But first, you drink."

Ato yelped as the hot, bitter liquid scalded his tongue. Marko's thumb stroked his throat, making sure he was swallowing.

"Again."

He took another scorching sip. Once more, Marko's fingers pressed lightly along his throat.

Satisfied, Marko grunted. "Okay, this not be poison. I give to Madam Eyra. Now go."

Ato fled as Marko padded out of his cabin to Eyra.

By the time he got back, Leslie was a nervous wreck, trying to hold Dzifa down. Hafsat was biting her nails to the flesh.

"You took so long!" Leslie was close to tears. "Dzifa was going to come after you. I had to fight her to stay!"

Ato breathlessly narrated his ordeal to his astonished friends.

"He locked you in? Goodness, you must have thought you were going to die," Hafsat whispered.

"But will he give it to her?" Dzifa asked.

Leslie looked worried. "Can we trust him? A man who walks around with a knife . . . instead of a stick or a cane?"

Ato did not know. He felt miserable and scared. They sat in silence, unsure of what to do next.

"We should go back," Leslie said. "Maybe we can finish off Mission Eight."

"But we need to know if he's given it to Eyra, and if she's better."

"Shh, footsteps," Hafsat whispered.

"You're hearing things," Dzifa began.

But Hafsat was right.

Richie had appeared behind them. He looked irritated.

"Gallant Geese. I've been worried about you." There was an edge to his tone. "Everyone got back to the Flocking Valley a while back."

Richie looked at Hafsat. "What's wrong?" His voice softened.

"There's something wrong with Eyra," Hafsat burst out.

He squatted and looked up at her, a furrow across his brow. "You've seen her?"

Hafsat nodded. "And she's talking strangely."

Richie folded his arms across his chest. A puzzled look crossed his face. "I thought so myself," he murmured half to himself, straightening up.

Richie took hold of Ato's hand. "I told the other Guardians," he said. His grip on Ato did not slacken. "I told them something was wrong. But some people think it's just Eyra being Eyra."

Ato exchanged a relieved glance with Dzifa. So all along Richie had known there was something odd about Eyra! But why had he kept telling them she was busy? Because he wanted to hide her strange behavior from them? Because he hadn't wanted them to see Eyra like that? Ato felt as if a weight had been lifted off him; Richie felt the same way they did!

"I don't get it," Richie continued. "She falls into these strange moods and she speaks like she's someone else. And when she's like that . . ." He looked bewildered. "There's nothing anyone can do. I can't think what the matter is. What she needs is a good doctor. Sometimes I think running this island becomes too much for her."

"Ato's grandmother said a flower was controlling her brain," Hafsat said.

Ato tensed. Nana had said not to tell anyone.

Richie's hand tightened around Ato's. "Really?" He looked at them intently, his gaze traveling from one face to another, finally resting back on Ato's.

"Ato, I heard Eyra talk about your grandmother's wisdom.

Maybe we should hear what she has to say. Heaven knows we need all the wisdom we can get to help Eyra."

Ato hesitated, not sure what to say. Tell *no one*, Nana had said.

Richie seemed to notice his hesitation. "It's okay, Ato, you can tell me anything," the Guardian said reassuringly. "Hafsat knows that."

Leslie and Dzifa looked curiously at Hafsat, but Ato understood. Richie knew about Hafsat's dad.

Richie's voice took on a concerned tone. "Listen, guys, let me be straight with you. The last time Eyra took a weird turn like this, it took ages to wear off. Five years, in fact. It's the main reason Nnoma has been closed. We were hoping it wouldn't happen again. I keep coming to her cabin to keep an eye on her and to make sure she's not getting worse. So I think we *really* need to hear what your grandmother thinks, Ato. It could help us to help Eyra."

A movement from the direction of the lake caught Ato's attention: a boat was approaching the mooring bay. He could see four, maybe five people in the boat. This was unusual. Wasn't Nnoma closed to visitors?

Richie saw them too. He glanced from them back to Eyra's cabin, then gestured toward the storage hut behind them.

"Why don't we go and sit in here, and have a quiet chat about this, because I'm getting very uncomfortable with this Eyra business. Something has to be done about it. I just don't know what."

And suddenly he was herding them gently but firmly toward the small stick hut.

Ato held back. "Can we go back to Mission Eight, Richie? There's not much time left, and we still have a chance to make it to the top three!"

His three friends raised their voices in agreement.

Richie studied them for a moment. Then, with one sweeping, unexpected move of his powerful arms, he shoved back all the Gallant Geese, sending them tumbling into the small hut.

CHAPTER TWENTY-EIGHT

ATO WAS SHOCKED INTO SILENCE BY RICHIE'S ROUGHNESS. The Guardian shut the door and turned around to face them. The hut was warm and windowless, but multiple rays of light filtered in through the sticks and reeds that made up the wall. Ato could still see everyone clearly. Why had Richie shoved them in here?

Richie pressed a hand to his heart.

Ato froze. He glanced at Dzifa. She too stood stock-still, staring at Richie's hand. At the dark bruise. It was shaped in the unmistakable curve of teeth marks.

"Richie?" Ato looked directly at the Guardian, afraid to look again at the bite marks in full view on his hand, unable to believe they were actually there. Richie's eyes were cool and steady. Ato's mind was anything but steady. The person in the corner of the garden yesterday was Richie!

"Your mother should have taught you not to bite, Ato." Richie leaned back against the rough wooden door. Gone was the sudden harshness in his tone. He spoke softly. Thoughtfully.

"Children. Nnoma is your playground. You come here to have

fun, run around, eat, and play. We Guardians trot after you, look after you, play your games. You go back and forget about Nnoma. But we stay, year in and year out. This is our home. We were born on the lands around here. We have nowhere else to go."

What was he talking about? Ato could see his friends were as baffled as he was.

"We won't forget about Nnoma," Dzifa said half-indignantly.

"You will!"

Ato shrank back. Why did Richie sound mad at them?

Richie breathed in deeply as if he were calming himself down. "You will forget," he said sadly. "You all do. And what happens to us when you leave? To us, the Guardians? Nothing. Nothing changes."

Bitterness crept into his voice. "Guardians, we're called. Guardians guard a treasure. And you know what, it's about time the Guardians enjoyed that treasure! Do you know what life was like for us, we who grew up across the lake from Nnoma? We walked three miles to school and back every day. We wore sandals with holes and oversized hand-me-down shorts. My father sold coconuts for a living when I was a child. After buyers ate the flesh and drank the water, my father sold the leftover husks for a few coins. He *still* sells husks for nothing." His tone hardened. "I want payback for my poor childhood. Payback for me, and for all of us who live around Nnoma."

By now sweat dribbled down Ato's temples and nose. He felt helpless and trapped. And Richie was not making any sense.

"I don't understand," Dzifa said. "What are you talking about?"

"You don't need to understand." Richie peered at the lake

through the gaps in the stick walls. "Eyra has changed her mind about Nnoma. Soon this island will be different. No more kids."

Nnoma would be different. Ato frowned. His mind ticked furiously, trying to recall where he had heard this. It hit him—at dinner with Eyra!

I have heard whispers, things about Nnoma that people want done differently. But their reasons are for the good of just a few people, not for the good of all people.

Through the slats of the hut, Ato could see down to the lakeshore. Three men and a woman had stepped out of the boat. Eyra had said Nnoma was closed to everybody but them. So who were these people? A Guardian in a green-and-blue Nnoma T-shirt was down with them, talking to them. It was too far away to tell who it was. Was it Kai? he thought frantically. His teammates had seen them too.

"Why won't there be kids on Nnoma? Eyra wouldn't change her mind about that," Dzifa protested.

Richie shrugged. "People change their minds all the time. And Eyra is just as much a person as anyone else. She *is* changing her mind, like the sensible person she is."

Ato gripped Dzifa's hand. Something was very wrong with Richie's words. Suddenly everything Nana had said made sense.

"You!" he burst out. "*You* want Eyra to do things differently. *You're* poisoning her mind. With the flower! You're controlling her! You're making her change her mind!"

Hafsat gasped.

Richie looked at him pityingly. "Change. Let me tell you

about change, Ato. Some of us have worked here for years earning pennies because Eyra wants to change the world. Well, now people are talking to her, smart people with smart plans. People who care about us. Who know what's best for those of us who live here. And now Eyra's changed her mind. So you see, there will be no more children on Nnoma! Lice . . . all of you! Crawling over the island, wasting my time! No more of you little maggots for me."

Hafsat looked frozen in shock.

Ato struggled to absorb the Guardian's venomous words. All this time he'd been smiling with Flock Eleven, he'd just been pretending? And he remembered Richie saying the same thing in his argument with Kai that rainy night on Rockside!

Dzifa seemed to have lost all her fear by now. "No, we don't see! Nnoma is for everyone, including children!"

"Of course you don't." He smiled. "You're kids. You see the sun reflecting like gold off the lake." He leaned forward. His eyes narrowed. "Well, I see a mountain of gold waiting to be found. Eyra sees it too. Now I have to go. There is serious business waiting for us."

Ato's mind was racing. He still didn't understand what Richie meant by gold, but he was sure Eyra wouldn't agree with Richie's talk about no more children. Was that what he and Kai had argued about that night? Was this why Kai had sounded so angry? He desperately hoped Marko had given Eyra Nana's drink. Had she drunk it? And if she had, was it working?

Ato pointed a quaking finger at Richie. "Don't! Don't make her do anything she doesn't want!"

"Shush." Richie's voice was controlled, menacing.

Fear tingled down Ato's spine.

"Be quiet. People will hear you; important people. And they're not as nice as I am. Nnoma is a big place. You'd be surprised at the unfortunate accidents that can happen to children on an island like this." Richie chuckled slyly. "I don't want any disturbances. I need to take our guests to Eyra." He smiled. "She can't wait to see them."

Ato felt his throat closing up in panic. He wanted Nana. He wanted his mother. He wanted the safety of his tiny home.

Leslie finally found his voice; it was a shrill, anxious one. "Please let us out, Richie."

"No. You'll stay safely locked in here until the businessmen have finished their discussion with Eyra and everything has been signed. I'll be back to let you out and then you can tell everyone that Eyra has changed her mind about Nnoma."

He unlatched the door and opened it. Bright light streamed in with a gust of cool air. "And, oh." He began turning to them. "I would advise you not to say anything to anyone about flowers. That's absolute nonsense. No one will believe y—" He did not finish his sentence.

Ato saw a blur as Leslie dived at Richie. There was a long hiss. The acrid smell of pepper spray filled the air. Richie let out a roar of pain. Cursing and coughing, he let go of the door and slapped one hand over his face, swinging out the other thick arm. Leslie ducked and Richie grabbed Ato's shoulder instead. Leslie sprayed again. This time Richie went down. He clapped both hands over his eyes, clawing at them. Ato's eyes and throat were on fire. Free from Richie's grasp, he leapt backward, knocking Hafsat over. She fell to the floor whimpering. Ato coughed painfully.

"*Aaargh*," Richie groaned, both hands still over his eyes. "Water," he croaked. "Water!"

But Leslie had shot out the door. Ato and Dzifa flew out after him. A few steps from the hut, Ato whirled around. He had to lock the door. Then he saw her.

"Hafsat!"

She was still in the hut, her anguished gaze on Richie, who was still on all fours, groaning.

"Come on, Hafsat!" Ato yelled.

"Richie," she sobbed. "He's hurt."

"What?" Dzifa's face was distorted with disbelief. "Let's go!"

"But we can't leave him. He's my friend! He needs water . . . for his eyes!"

"C'mon, Ato!" Dzifa grabbed his arm.

He yanked it free and ran over to Hafsat, clamping his hand around her wrist and hauling her out. Then he kicked the door of the hut shut and rammed the flimsy lock in place.

CHAPTER TWENTY-NINE

"THAT LOCK IS NOTHING! HE'LL BE COMING FOR US!" LESLIE wailed as they ran.

Ato's legs, aching from his mountain climb, flew across the ground. His eyes still stung. He kept a firm hold on Hafsat's hand and glanced behind him as they ran. No sign of Richie. He was still inside the cabin. Dzifa was several strides ahead. Keeping a hold on Hafsat was like running with a lead ball chained to his wrist; she was pulling back.

"Hafsat, let's go!" he yelled, yanking her forward in frustration.

"Go where?" she cried.

"Away. Go away from here!" Leslie was running faster than Ato had ever seen.

They covered the next few hundred yards in blind panic, instinctively running down the path that led toward Rockside. It felt like the safest thing to do. If he did get out, Richie would probably head to Cabinside to look for them.

Ato yanked again on Hafsat's hand to speed her up. She cried out in pain. Dzifa whipped her head around to see what was happening. Her foot hit a jutting stone, sending her flying headlong. She skidded tummy-down over the rough ground, coming to a stop a few feet away from where she had stumbled.

"Owww!" She sat up and clutched her legs. Ato ran up to her. She had scraped her palms, both knees, and her shins badly. Dark red blood was already trickling down both legs.

"Oh gosh. You're hurt! Leslie!" he called, as loudly as he dared.

Leslie slowed down and looked back.

Ato gestured wildly. "Come back!" He pointed to Dzifa, who had struggled to her feet and straightened up. She was clearly in pain.

Leslie pounded back to them, huffing and wheezing, but still looking like he could sprint another mile if he needed to.

"Leslie," Ato panted, glancing back to make sure no one was on their heels. "We can't keep running. Dzifa is hurt."

"But we can't stay here!" Leslie exclaimed, aghast. "Someone will hear Richie and rescue him. We have to keep moving!"

He was about to take off again, but Ato grabbed his sleeve. Leslie tried to wrest himself free. Ato tackled him to the rough ground and sat on his chest.

"Leslie! Hold up! Look, the pit we found the other day is in that direction. All we need now is for one of us to fall into it and it'll be all over."

A dozen lights flashed like a fireworks display in his head. The lights imploded into a single startling idea that depended on several things working together at the same time. Could they do it?

There's a reason you have that power. The power to see what you want even when you don't actually have it. Trust that power.

At the memory of Nana's words, energy surged through his sore body. He changed his mind.

"Let's keep going that way." He pointed ahead toward the rocks and the giant aloe. His idea was riddled with holes. Literally. But he had to try.

"But the pit is there!" Hafsat said.

"We know that. Richie doesn't."

Silence hung in the warm air for a moment after Ato had spoken.

Dzifa spoke slowly. "You want Richie in the pit."

"Yes."

Hafsat gave a squeak of disbelief.

Ato held her hand tightly. "Hafsat. You're on our team, not Richie's. I know Richie's been great to you, and we haven't always been the best teammates to each other. But look at what he's doing! You believed my grandmother when she said something was controlling Eyra. That's why you helped us find everything we needed so fast. Now you've got to believe this. Richie is controlling Eyra because he wants to make her do something she doesn't want to!"

"What does he want her to do?" Hafsat asked, doubt in her eyes.

"I dunno. Something about no children here, and gold. You were there!" Ato said.

"It doesn't make sense to us. But we know Eyra doesn't want to do it. We can't trust *him*. We've got to stop him! Hafsat, do you believe him or us?" Dzifa exclaimed.

Hafsat was visibly quaking.

"How are we going to get him into the hole?" Perspiration trickled down Leslie's face as he spoke.

Ato's words tumbled out fast and shakily. "First, we've got to let him know we're here. Then one of us has to lead him in that direction, toward the hole. It's around the bend, by the giant aloe. *We* know it's exactly three long steps around the bend and then a jump. One of us jumps across, Richie runs after them. If he's running fast I don't think he'll see the hole in time."

"Risky. But it might work." Dzifa's face was contorted with pain. "One of us runs toward the hole and jumps. Richie runs after the person. He falls into the hole. But let me get this straight: Who's jumping?"

"Leslie."

Leslie let out a sound like that of a trapped kitten. "You brought me here to die!"

Ato pulled his friend to his feet.

"Dzifa's hurt. Leslie, you've got to make that jump. Then I can run up and get help."

Leslie clutched Ato's throat, almost strangling him. "Help? Here?"

"No, not here. I have to make a call!"

"To who?"

"Max!"

"*Our* Max? The reporter? What for? He's miles away!" Leslie wailed.

"You heard what Richie said. He's got people here already. When Eyra signs what they have, there will be no more children on Nnoma and Richie will get his gold. So he's poisoning Eyra's mind, like how the Prophet of Fire put poison in our pond to get rid of the farmers."

Hafsat's eyes went wide. She raised trembling fists to her face. "I . . . my . . ." she began, but her voice seemed to dry up.

"That's a crime, controlling Eyra's mind to make her sign something!" Dzifa burst out.

"Yes, and that's why maybe Max can get us help with that! So that somebody stops Richie! You can do this, Leslie!" Ato's throat throbbed with urgency.

Leslie took a step back. "It sounds easy, until Richie jumps across too. And he'll be so mad by then. He'll kill us—me first for pepper-spraying him. Then he'll throw our bodies into his lake of gold."

"He'll have to catch us first," Ato said.

"Hafsat!" Richie's insistent voice traveled downwind to them.

They froze. Fear snaked around Ato's heart. Through his pepper-sprayed eyes, Richie must have peered through the hut walls and realized they were not running toward the cabins. He was not going to give up. If he could give a brain-controlling flower to Eyra, what would he do to them?

"Quick." Ato pointed to the giant aloe. They scurried toward it. They were now within a few feet of the hole.

"Hafsaa-aaa-aat!" Richie called again.

Ato huddled behind the gigantic spiky plant. Dzifa squeezed his arm. Her hand felt clammy. Hafsat was breathing fast. Too fast. It sounded like she was struggling for air.

"Where are you? Hafsat!" Richie's voice was closer, strong and commanding. "Kids, come on out! You don't understand! It's okay. I won't hurt you!"

"I need to get to the Chirp and Chatter now!" Ato breathed. He would have to make his way uphill, but at least Richie wouldn't see him.

Leslie clutched his shoulder. "Ato, Max can't help us here! We're on our own."

Ato grabbed his hand. "Leslie, do something! Richie must know you're here!"

"Hafsat! Ato! Dzifa! Leslie! Come here! Now!"

Ato shuddered. "I've got to go."

"All right . . ." Leslie whispered.

"Richie!" Hafsat's shrill voice pierced the air. Ato almost choked. Dzifa and Leslie gasped, horrified.

Ato clapped his hand over Hafsat's mouth. "What's wrong with you!" he whispered, shaking.

She tore his hand away. "Richie!" she screamed again. She turned to them. "Hide," she whispered. "*I'll* jump!"

"No! You can't ju—" Dzifa breathed.

But Hafsat was gone. She darted off toward the sound of Richie's voice. The three others lay flat behind the giant aloe, hidden from view by the huge hydra-shaped plant, and unable to see anything beyond it.

Leslie wrung his hands. "I was going to jump. Now she's going to bring him back here to us."

Dzifa covered her face and groaned.

The sound of footsteps pounding in their direction filled Ato's heart with dread.

Richie gave a yell, loud and angry.

Now there were two sets of footsteps. Hafsat was running. Richie was running faster. He was chasing her.

Hafsat was slow, Ato thought desperately. And she could never get across the hole. His plan was ruined now. It was over.

A loud yell ripped through the air.

Ato's heart began a frantic beat.

"He's got her. He's going to get us too! Let's go!" Leslie begged.

They peered out from behind the aloe, and Ato gripped Leslie. A figure had emerged.

"Wha-aa-at?" Ato breathed.

It was Hafsat, stumbling toward them.

Ato stared at her, afraid to ask the big question. Wordlessly, she nodded. They stood in silence, stunned at what had just happened. It had worked! Thanks to Hafsat, Richie was trapped.

Dzifa's mouth opened and closed as if she were a fish in a bowl. "You . . . you *jumped*? Wow. Just . . . wow," she finished weakly.

Ato felt exactly the same way. Dzifa flung her arms around Hafsat.

Hafsat drew back. "Richie is my friend. But just now, when you talked about the Prophet, I remembered something my dad said when I spoke to him on the phone. He's in the same prison as your Prophet of Fire . . . Yakayaka. And I think Richie knows the Prophet."

CHAPTER THIRTY

"*What?*" Ato, Leslie, and Dzifa exclaimed together.

But Hafsat had no chance to say any more.

"Hafsat! Ato!"

Ato jumped at Richie's voice. It sounded muffled, but still loud enough to be heard from a distance. It also sounded furious.

"Guys," Ato said quickly. "Now the other Guardians will be looking for us. And someone *will* hear him."

"We've got to get moving," Dzifa said. "Lead them away from you, Ato, so you don't get caught. And Eyra—we have to protect her!"

Ato nodded quickly. "What are you going to do?"

"Leave that to me."

Dzifa took Hafsat's and Leslie's hands in hers. "I mean, leave that to us. We're a great team. Let's see how much we can mess things up for Richie before he gets out."

Ato flew up the path and through the thickly wooded section of the slope around and behind the cabins, and toward the Chirp and Chatter, trampling through the undergrowth and sending startled lizards and bush mice springing in all directions. He hoped his friends would be okay. That Richie would not leap out of the pit and grab them. He hoped there would be no Guardians in the Chirp and Chatter looking for him. And he hoped his idea would work.

Please, God, please, God, please, God. His two-word prayer was in frantic rhythm with his footsteps.

When he ran into the Chirp and Chatter, Clara was watching a little dog cycling on the wide curved TV. The TV was on maximum volume. To his immense relief, all she did was express surprise at seeing him again so quickly. She smiled sweetly at him and handed him a phone.

Phone pressed to his ear, he walked a few steps across to a window facing the lake. The first rings went unanswered. He tried again, with trembling fingers, hoping he had gotten the number right. This time a familiar voice answered.

"Hello?"

Ato could have wept with relief. "Max! Oh thank God you answered!"

"Hey, kiddo!" There was genuine pleasure in the ace reporter's voice. "Great to hear from you. Didn't think you'd remember your old buddy while you were flapping around in bird paradise. Just on my way to this big story, and—"

"Max. You've gotta help me. Listen." At top speed, he poured out his story, adding Hafsat's message.

Max listened in silence. "Kid, that's not much to go on," he said slowly. "I've got a reputation for the truth."

Ato clutched the phone with cold hands. "Please, Max. Remember who helped you get that first story, the one that made you big?"

More silence. After a few excruciating seconds, Max exhaled slowly.

"You've got to help me stop this. Call my grandmother. She knows something, but she's not telling me. Please, Max! Plea—"

A shadow loomed behind him and the phone was snatched from his hand. He spun around.

Kai. And she looked ready to devour him.

"What is wrong with you kids?" She grabbed his shoulders with both hands and looked like she was holding back from shaking him like a rattle. Her frog eyes flashed her wrath. "Your teammates are running around screaming crazy things about Richie controlling Eyra's mind!"

Just as suddenly, she pushed him away and placed her hands on her head. "What's wrong with everyone? There are strangers on the island and I don't know what they are doing here. Eyra will not be happy about that, but Eyra is . . . she's losing it . . . aaaargh!" She clenched one fist as if she wanted to box someone.

Ato took a step back, and she grabbed his shoulder again. Clara scurried up and placed a soothing hand on Kai's arm. Kai smacked her hand away. She shook her head in frustration. "Clara, I'm trying to hold things together. But . . ." She spread out one hand in a gesture that seemed to be one of genuine helplessness.

A thought flashed through Ato's mind. Kai's argument with

Richie. Could it have been about this? He didn't know if Max was going to help, if he even could. Could Kai help?

"Kai—" he began.

The beep-beep of her phone interrupted him.

"Richie?" she growled, holding it to her ear. Ato tried to wriggle away. Her grasp on him tightened.

"Yes, he's here." She turned stupefied eyes to Ato. "Okay, I'll hold on to him." Ato strained to free himself. It was like trying to crack himself out of concrete. What had Richie done to his friends? And what about Eyra?

Kai lowered her phone. "Ato, you tricked Richie into a *pit*? Are you out of your mind?" Lines of incredulity rippled across her forehead. "Somebody needs to tell me what madness is sweeping over this island. Everyone is mad, from Eyra right down to you kids. In all my years I have never—"

"Kai!" Ato allowed his gut feeling to push him. After all, that night on Rockside, she had disagreed with Richie. Maybe she would hear what he had to say and help them. "Kai, there's a plot. To stop kids from coming to Nnoma! Richie was talking about that, and mountains of gold, and other stuff!"

Behind him, Clara gave a cry of alarm.

Kai gasped. "Eyra would never allow that!"

But Ato could tell Kai was scared.

"So someone drugged her. Poisoned her! They gave her a flower drink, to change her mind. Please believe me, Kai. You've got to help us help Eyra." Even as he spoke, the frightening thought occurred to him that it was possibly too late.

"They drugged . . . ? They did what? Who is they?" Kai demanded.

"Richie . . . he gave her the flower, because some people are coming and he wants her to sign something so Nnoma will be different, with no more children. And he said something about life being better now for people around Nnoma!"

Kai's face was taut. "This is what she . . . we had always been afraid of . . ." Her eyes narrowed. "Richie? I don't believe it. I don't believe you." She grabbed both his wrists. "You're lying! You're staying with me until I find out what's going on!"

Behind them, Clara looked as if she wanted to run away.

"It's true!" He could not free himself from her grip. Max, he thought. It had been several minutes since he'd spoken to the reporter. Could he help? Would he?

CHAPTER THIRTY-ONE

From outside came the sound of charging footsteps. A second later Richie and Koku burst into the room. Their clothes were disheveled and they were coated in brown dust from their heads to their shoes. Ato's jaw quivered at the fury on Richie's face.

"Richie?" Kai's voice was questioning. "What are these wild stories? Why are the kids running around . . . ?"

Richie did not answer her. Instead, he turned to Clara. "Did he make a call?"

Clara nodded.

"Which phone?"

Clara thrust it at him. She looked terrified, as if she had been accused of stealing it.

"Thanks," he said curtly. "Now leave."

Clara nodded quickly and scurried out the door nearest to her.

Richie pinned Ato down with cold, angry eyes. "Don't look at me like that, Ato. I would never hurt you. But I can't allow you to go running around scaring the other kids with wild stories. Now tell me, Ato, who did you speak to?"

"No one, Richie." He answered quickly. Too quickly.

Richie tapped the phone twice. The call was answered immediately. It was on speaker setting.

"Ato?"

"Hello." Richie spoke in a level voice. "This is Nnoma. May I know who this is?"

"Hello, Nnoma. This is Maximilian. Call me Max."

Richie shot Ato a steely glance. His heart sank.

"Max, I'm guessing Ato called you?"

"Yes, he did, Mr. Nnoma," Max said. His tone was brisk as usual.

"We have a problem with him. He's playing silly games, spreading stuff about other people. Scaring kids with wild stories. We're getting him to see a doctor soon. What did he tell you?"

Max's voice was loud and clear over the phone. "Nothing that made sense. To be honest, I barely listened. I figured straightaway that it was his idea of a prank. You know what kids are like." He gave a laugh that sounded like a dry bark. "So if that's all, I have actual, real business to attend to now. Gotta go."

The line went dead.

Anguish seared through Ato. Max did not believe him! He gave a violent tug, wrenched himself out of Kai's grasp, and took off toward the opposite door at the Chirp and Chatter.

"Catch him!" Richie roared to Koku.

Koku sprinted after him. Ato ran out the door, spun to the right, and in instant decision dived behind the door and the stack of huge floor cushions. Koku burst through the doorway, looked around wildly, and took off around the building. Ato huddled as close to the red-tiled floor as he could. What would his next move be? Would Koku keep running, looking for him? Would he come back? He pressed against the wall. He knew he would not be seen if he stayed put. He dared to peek into the Chirp and Chatter through a crack in the doorway. He could see Richie clearly.

"Kai, join us! Eyra is going to sign soon. Nnoma can be greater than it is now!" Richie leaned toward Kai, speaking in a tone of urgency.

"You disappoint me, Richie. Nnoma is already great," Kai said stiffly.

"Kai, look around! You and I started here together! We were teenagers. Is this really what you want? Having the Flocks coming here to run around, then leaving this place and forgetting us? How many Flocks have passed through our hands? How many still keep in touch?"

Kai paced up and down the room. "But all around the world they're changing the way people live with nature. That's what they're supposed to do—make a difference where they are. They don't need to keep in touch!"

"They've forgotten about Nnoma! They're all out there thinking about getting rich. We were young when Eyra made us an offer to be Guardians. We thought it was good. Our simple village minds were happy. Now I see it's stupid to just stay here. You saw how people who came to dig for wealth buried in *our* earth became rich. But we didn't!"

"Is that what you'll do to Nnoma? Mine that beautiful mountain for what is there? Rip away the soil and trees? Turn the lake and streams into mud bowls? Drive every living thing away? What happened to you, Richie?" Kai cried.

Richie pounded one fist into his palm. "I can't keep caring about the world and these birds. What about us, huh? They don't care about us, so *we* need to look after ourselves. Do you want to stay here and stay poor? Don't you want all that wealth?"

"No, I don't!" she spat. "I want to be able to drink straight from the river in the village our grandmothers came from! Remember we used to do that when we were children, before the big machines came and tore up the trees? Remember how, after that, nothing could grow anymore—no fruit, no vegetables? There was no more shade, just heat and rocks and dust. Remember the pits of muddy water they left behind? The schoolteacher whose son drowned in it?"

Richie stood stony-faced, watching Kai.

"And the dust," Kai wailed. "Oh, the dust everywhere! Our grandmothers began coughing all the time and had such painful breathing and irritated eyes." She shook her head. "Those machines blasting the hills, truck after truck, carrying away the soil from underneath our feet and our grandmothers' homes, carrying it all away until nothing was left but rubble and holes in the ground!"

Richie leaned toward her, his eyes glittering. "You know what those trucks were carrying away? Money! Beautiful homes! Fine cars! Luxury holidays! And our grandmothers and everyone else stood by and left us poor. I won't let that happen. If we don't take the gold in Nnoma's mountain, someone else will, Kai. It's only a matter of time!"

Behind the cushions, Ato remained in a tense, silent curl. There was gold in Nnoma's mountain . . . so that was what this was about!

"Richie, if you didn't believe in Nnoma, then——" Kai began.

"Oh, I believe in Nnoma! I believe in a Nnoma that will make us rich. Not a Nnoma for kids who go back into the world and forget about this place."

"They don't forget!" she burst out.

"Five years we stayed idle! Earning pennies while Eyra slept on a gold mine! Enough, Kai! The rest of our lives are for us!"

Ato stayed frozen in position, watching the heated exchange.

"That's not what Nnoma is about. If you wanted to be rich, why don't you just quit?" Her tone was anguished but defiant.

"I'm not quitting. It's our time! The land we come from has to look after us too. Look at the birds we have here, all the rare ones. Do you know how much people will pay to own one of them? And we can always breed some more!"

Kai looked close to weeping. "Richie, the more people buy them, the more others will see them and want them too. It's never enough. You should not be working here if you don't believe this."

"When we were children, the first thing beyond our village we could see was the Dawn Locus and Nnoma. We have looked after Nnoma, and now Nnoma can look after us." He took her hands. "Join us, Kai. The businesspeople are here, waiting for me. Eyra is going to sign, then so will I. A good part of the gold they find will come to me and to all those who have been loyal to this cause. Once that boy has been caught, the island will be quiet and the deal will be done!"

"They will take everything from Nnoma and then the island will die," Kai said brokenly. "Just like our villages."

Richie shrugged. "We all die, Kai. Us. Nnoma. Nothing lasts forever. Even the sun will die one day. Before then, we need to take what we can."

Kai's shoulders sagged. It seemed as if her fight and spirit had left her. "Oh, Richie!" Her voice cracked. "How can you talk like that? How do you think you will get away with doing this . . . this thing that Eyra has always feared?"

He smiled knowingly. "Well, she made it easy for us. She's good at keeping quiet."

Kai stepped back, shaking her head. Her voice was sorrowful. "I thought you knew me, Richie. You really think I will stand by and watch this happen? I'll do everything to stop you!"

Richie was silent. Then a look of remorse crept across his face. He hung his head and looked at the floor. "You're right, Kai. I don't know what's come over me." He sighed long and deep. "Let's sit for a moment," he said, waving toward two chairs nearby. "Here, have some coconut water, and let's think about this again." He unhooked his flask and handed it to her.

Kai took the flask. "This is awful business for Nnoma and for everything that lives here, and even beyond here. I need you to understand that."

She tipped her head back and took a long drink. Richie

watched her closely. She lowered the flask and sighed. Several seconds passed. Still, Kai sat, holding the flask in silence. After a couple of minutes Richie smiled and took the flask from her unresisting hands.

"Kai," he said softly.

"Yes, Richie." Her voice was flat.

"Kai, It's time for change. Say it."

"It's time for change," she echoed. Still the same flat tone. There was no passion, no anger. There was an emptiness to her voice that sent a cold ripple down Ato's spine. Kai had become like Eyra!

"We will make it different," he said.

Ato watched in horror as Kai repeated after Richie. "We will make it different."

"No more children," he said.

"No more children." She looked straight ahead.

Richie smiled and rose to his feet. "That's a good girl," he murmured. "The boy's grandmother knows the power of this flower. Now let's just wait here. The other kids will be taken care of. Koku will be back with the boy, and then he'll have a taste of this nectar."

Ato's blood froze within his veins.

CHAPTER THIRTY-TWO

"Now *you* listen to me, Kai." Richie's tone was relaxed and chatty. "We'll kick these kids off the island, and then when we get our money from mining the gold on Nnoma, we'll buy another island somewhere else. We'll buy birds and put them there, but this time it won't all be for children—only the wealthy and worthy. We'll have luxury cabins. Huge. At the top floor of each, there'll be a balcony, and you'll have an all-around view of the island. Say it with me."

"All-around view of the island," she repeated obediently.

Richie leaned back with one arm dangling over the back of his chair. Ato listened in increasing horror as Richie's voice thickened with excitement.

"You'll love it! The cabins will be modern, with hot tubs, saunas, private butlers, armchairs so luxurious you could get lost in them! What a wonderful dream! Nnoma is our golden goose, Kai, and we're going to squeeze every last shining egg out of her to make this dream come true." He sighed with pleasure and stretched forward to take Kai's hand. "Tell me, Kai, that would be wonderful, wouldn't it?"

Kai nodded woodenly. "Yes, that would be wonderful, Richie."

He nodded his approval. "You're a fast learner, like Eyra."

Nana had been so horribly right. The flower was being used to control Eyra's mind, and now Kai's. They couldn't think for themselves! And Richie wanted to use it on him! Had Richie already used it on his friends?

Ato was trembling. How could he have thought he could get the better of Richie? Wild plans only worked in movies and in stories. In real life, adults were smarter and they always got their way. Kids like him always ended up losing. A wave of despair washed over him. Then he stiffened. Voices in the distance. The sound of children. They were yelling and screaming. His blood ran cold. What was going on?

Then he heard another sound, this time very close. Footsteps! A few people were running to the Chirp and Chatter. Fast. He clenched his fists so tightly, his nails cut into his palm. He flinched as the door on the far end of the room banged open. Richie leapt to his feet as Koku, Frank the Tank, and Bea rushed in.

"The children!" Frank panted. "The children . . ."

Ato's chattering teeth pressed into his lip. Which children? Were Dzifa, Leslie, and Hafsat all right? What about everyone else?

"On TV! Change the channel! Sunshine TV!" Koku shouted.

Bea threw her phone at Richie. "People are calling! The phone won't stop ringing!"

With shaky hands, Koku grabbed the remote control from

Clara's desk and pressed a button. Ato peeked through a crack in the cushions. The TV channel changed. He watched the huge screen in amazement as the headlines flashed:

NNOMA OWNER DRUGGED: KIDS OUT, MINING CROOKS IN? CRIMINALS PLOT TO TURN BIRD PARADISE INTO ENVIRONMENTAL HELL

"What? That boy! That man! They . . . he . . . !" Richie spluttered. He stood transfixed as the Sunshine TV jingle played and a newscaster wearing a purple blouse with a matching shade of lipstick appeared. She spoke clearly and crisply.

"Information reaching Sunshine says criminals have drugged the owner of Nnoma in a plot to hunt for gold on the bird paradise! This was disclosed by our very own Maximilian Odum, who broke the shocking news of the Prophet of Fire earlier this year. According to Max, a little over half an hour ago, reliable sources on Nnoma uncovered a sinister plot to take over the exclusive bird paradise by criminal means."

The newscaster pursed her purple lips disapprovingly and frowned at the camera. "In what turns out to be a closely guarded secret, the bird paradise is not only rich in flora and fauna, but has rich gold veins in its mountain. In addition, the soil just beneath its wooded hillsides is rich in bauxite. This information has been kept highly confidential for many years, in order to protect the environmental paradise from treasure hunters. Max, can you come in?"

"We have to go!" Bea implored, but Richie stood rooted, staring at the screen with bulging eyes. Kai sat looking blankly at them.

Max's serious face appeared on the screen. "My trustworthy informant relayed a message about a plot that is currently under way. It appears, shockingly, that criminal agents have drugged the owner of Nnoma in a ploy to make her sign a dubious deal. This deal will allow businessmen to blast through the island's mountain in the hunt for gold.

"Nnoma is an unspoiled private island, a rare jewel in the lake region," he continued. His level voice still carried a sense of urgency. "Its name, Nnoma, is from the Akan word for bird: anoma. As far back as any person around here can remember, Nnoma has been a migration rest point for hundreds of bird species.

"Nnoma's owner, Eyra, inherited the island from her wealthy father and has faithfully preserved its purity. Ten years ago, she began a select program allowing young people to visit the island. These young people, the best of whom are called Asafo, are trained to understand the importance of living in harmony with our planet. From here they go out to defend the natural world, wherever they are and however they can."

Richie clenched his fists and screamed an expletive.

The newscaster leaned forward and looked deep into the camera. "Max, what do we know about the drugging? And what will happen next?"

Ato watched Max's face tighten. "The owner of the island has possibly been betrayed, drugged by a close aide with poison from a flower on the island. We're talking about a serious crime here, and an environmental catastrophe if they get away with it. The Dawn Locus, Nnoma's iconic peak, could be reduced to a heap of rubble. There would be dust clouds, and the pristine lake waters would be polluted by chemicals such as arsenic. Thousands of animal species would vanish from the island, which would become a barren wasteland. The police have been informed and are taking swift action."

The newscaster nodded. "Thank you, Maximilian."

Max disappeared and the camera focused back on the grim-faced newscaster.

"The terms Asafo and Nnoma are trending on the internet," she said. "Social media platforms are on fire with outraged messages from Asafo. Social media influencers, ordinary citizens, and public figures alike are demanding an immediate investigation. Asafo are even urging people to gather in open squares and to march on the streets in order to get an investigation into the happenings on Nnoma. The news is going viral worldwide."

Richie threw his head back in fury and frustration. "Aaaaaargh! That boy! I'll . . . I'll . . . !"

With an explosive roar, Richie and his three Guardians raced out of the Chirp and Chatter, leaving Kai alone in the chair. Ato felt as limp as a rag. Bea! Frank the Tank! Koku! They were all in on it!

Scene after scene flashed on the screen showing Nnoma and the Dawn Locus.

"Nnoma is not a huge island," the newscaster continued. "Any suspects would not have gotten far. Acting on the information from Max's source, we are informed that police are heading to Nnoma in speedboats, along with a helicopter, to investigate the situation."

The scene changed and the newscaster began to report heavy flooding in a town in the Northern Region of Ghana.

Ato remained motionless, too terrified to emerge from his hiding place. What if they came back? What if they were waiting for him outside the Chirp and Chatter? Several excruciatingly long minutes ticked by. The sound of clamoring children carried on, chaotic and frightening. Had anyone been hurt? Or worse? Had the kids been given the flower poison to drink? Were they all zombies now?

He finally mustered up his courage and crept out from behind the cushions. The room was deserted, save for Kai. She sat on her chair staring ahead, her hands limply by her sides.

He hurried over to her. "Kai."

She looked at him as if she had never seen him before. "Yes."

He took her hand. "Come, Kai, let's go." She rose obediently and followed as he led her out as if she were a child. They walked down the wooded path and rounded the bend that overlooked the Flocking Valley. Ato inhaled sharply. Police were swarming up from the lake onto the island!

CHAPTER THIRTY-THREE

ALL THE OTHER SIXTY-THREE KIDS OF FLOCK ELEVEN HAD formed a human barricade around Eyra's cabin by the time Ato arrived. They were shouting at the top of their voices, shaking threatening fists and wielding branches. No one was allowed through, not even the Guardians.

"How did this happen!" a stupefied Ato yelled to Dzifa, Leslie, and Hafsat, who stood on the front line, Eyra's stone steps, brandishing long sticks. Leslie pointed to a familiar figure. He had both fists in the air, and was clearly the leader of the hollering, angry kids.

Ato's jaw slackened. "Bello?"

Dzifa nodded. "We met him while we were running up from Rockside screaming. I told him everything, what Richie was planning to do. And he stopped his mission at once! You should have seen him charging off, bellowing to all the kids to come and help protect Eyra!"

The tall boy glanced over at Ato. The dark determination on his face lifted. It was replaced by a grin of delight.

"Wow," Ato managed weakly. He took a step forward. Bello strode up to him. And the two boys embraced.

Ato stepped back first. "Thank you, Bello," he said humbly.

The caterpillar eyebrows jerked up and Bello smiled. "That's what falcons do, right? We move. Fast."

Ato laughed. He'd never thought he would find Bello's superior smile so welcoming.

The next hour was a blur. Ato stood in Eyra's garden with Flock Eleven and watched the police take over. Richie, Koku, Frank, Bea, and two other Guardians were arrested from the caves and led down to a police boat.

It turned out that Eyra had fallen into a deep sleep after drinking the potion Marko had boiled up. The police had checked her vital signs and were worried because she had not stirred. Kai too was in a zombie state and had been kept in Eyra's cabin. A doctor and water ambulance were on the way.

Ato swallowed his anxiety. He knew his friends were thinking what he was thinking: Had Nana's potion worked? Or could it have made Eyra worse?

The four important-looking men and women who had arrived earlier on Nnoma looked very agitated indeed. They sat at Eyra's table beneath the tree, ties loosened and jackets unbuttoned, answering police questions. Ato had overheard them protest their innocence; they didn't know Richie had no right to sell Nnoma. And as for Eyra being drugged, they shook their heads vigorously, swearing they knew nothing about it.

A policewoman behind Ato muttered to a colleague that she

didn't believe them. She also said she suspected someone else was behind the scenes.

Blood samples from Eyra and Kai were being sent off for laboratory tests. Ato knew what would show up. So did the police detective in charge of the team, a lean, tall man in a black uniform.

"This is pretty poison," the detective said, standing in front of the Gallant Geese with his thumbs hooked into his belt. A bunch of the innocent-looking purple flowers lay on a plastic sheet on the ground before him. "Brugmansia. Angel's trumpet. There are many names for it," he continued. "South America has a kind called borrachero. It's a very helpful plant, if you have dirty motives. After Eyra had been given a dose of that"—he shook his head grimly—"these crooks could get her to do anything. And the best—or worst—thing, depending on whether you're Richie or his victims—is that it punches huge holes in a person's memories."

"But my nana's medicine. Don't you think it can help Eyra and Kai?" Ato asked anxiously.

The detective shrugged. "We don't know how badly the poison has affected them. For many victims, afterward it's impossible for them to patch together a story that makes any sense. They might even forget everything."

The detective eyed the flowers again. "There were no worries about the bees detecting this one. They sniff out drugs, poisonous chemicals, stuff like that. The crooks found a way around that with homegrown poison. In a drink, this poison has no taste or smell."

He patted Ato on his shoulder, and the policeman's lean face cracked in a smile. "You did good, guys. You got the news out so fast. It exploded like a bomb. Started like a regular day for me, then the next thing I knew, some group called the Asafo were burning up the phone lines. I tell you, everyone out there now is shouting about saving Nnoma. Those Asafo are something else."

Despite their concern over Eyra, the Gallant Geese grinned at each other. Richie was wrong—the Asafo had not forgotten about Nnoma!

An officer called out to the chief detective from Eyra's cabin that the doctor and water ambulance had just arrived on Nnoma. The chief detective turned to go. "Let's keep our fingers crossed about Eyra and Kai. You did a great job, kids!" he said. He touched his forehead in a salute and strode off down to the lakeside.

Another detective came up to the Gallant Geese, sat them down, and began recording their account on a handheld device. Around them, Flock Eleven and the remaining ten Guardians—minus Kai—gathered around, listening in spellbound silence.

"After Richie fell into the pit, we ran screaming to Eyra's cabin," Dzifa began. She looked down at her bandaged legs and made a face. "Well, Leslie and Hafsat ran. I hobbled behind them."

"Then Bea and Frank the Tank came running to us," Hafsat said. Her face was streaked with dried sweat. "Everyone was looking for us, they said. And they kept telling us to calm down. That's when Kai came. She ordered Bea and Frank not to let anyone near us. And she took off to look for Ato."

Dzifa continued to tell how Richie had come running up from the pit, with Koku and two other Guardians who had helped to rescue him.

"So Richie called Kai's phone, and ran off to the Chirp and Chatter. He left Bea and Frank with us. They were being really nice. Bea offered us a flask of cold coconut water." Dzifa hung her head. "I nearly took it," she confessed. "I was hot and thirsty."

"But I said . . ." Leslie clamped his lips for a moment and shook his head. "I wasn't going to drink from a flask people had put their mouths all over."

"And Hafsat whispered to me not to drink it," Dzifa said. She turned to Hafsat, her eyes shining. "You're the best, Hafsat! I was wrong—it's a good thing Ato chose you for our team!" Dzifa chuckled. "And that's when we ran away from them, screaming about Eyra. We met Bello, and he got everyone in Flock Eleven to ditch Mission Eight and take over!"

So Richie had thought Dzifa, Leslie, and Hafsat would drink the flower drug, Ato realized. And if he had drunk it too, then that would have erased their memories! He shuddered at the thought. None of the Gallant Geese would have ever remembered what happened.

Dzifa had turned toward the lake. A team of grave-looking paramedics with two stretchers were hurrying up the hill, following the police detective to Eyra's cabin. Ato's heart constricted. Was she worse? What about Kai? Silence settled like a thick blanket over the children of Flock Eleven as they watched the team disappear into Eyra's cabin.

Moments later, Marko stumbled out of Eyra's cabin. Ato and his teammates ran over to him.

The cook reached for Ato's shoulder, his head hanging in

defeat. "I give her the drink." He sounded robbed of all hope. "The drink yous give me. She drink all. Like a child. And then she sleep. Not moving. So they taking her away."

Flock Eleven watched in dismay as the paramedics emerged with Eyra and Kai on stretchers and hurried down the hill. Moments later, the water ambulance sped off, bearing Eyra and Kai. There was still a good amount left of what he had boiled up for Eyra, Marko said. The police had taken it away.

The remaining Guardians urged Flock Eleven to stay calm and to cooperate with the police, who were in full action, interviewing Guardians and children, searching the island, and dusting Eyra's cabin for fingerprints.

Half an hour after Eyra and Kai had been taken away, Ato looked toward the setting sun and signaled discreetly to his teammates. There was something they had to do. And with everyone so distracted by what had happened, this was the best time to do it.

CHAPTER THIRTY-FOUR

THEY STOLE AWAY FROM THE EXCITEMENT, DOWN EYRA'S steps, to the path that led past their cabins.

"Where are we going?" Dzifa groaned. "My knees hurt. We're walking so fast!"

Ato scrabbled down a bank of loose stones and turned to help her down. "Just come with me. Please. Don't ask me anything, because I don't know . . . I just think . . ."

"I get it," she said. "It's about the plan. Cool. Let's go."

Ato's heart was up in his throat. He'd always imagined being a falcon: killer hunting instinct, locking onto a target, chasing it down with blinding speed.

But for the first time, as he approached his target, he felt like a goose. Geese flew in a flock. They traveled miles and miles to a destination, guided by instinct and by a compass in their heads. He too was flying with his team, following his gut instinct and a compass in his heart. Would he find his father's plan?

A light breeze from the lake cooled his perspiring face. This was their last evening on Nnoma. He prayed he was right. If he wasn't . . . he didn't want to think about that. Maybe much later another kid might find it. The thought stabbed his heart, and he pushed it away. Was this just another wild goose chase? He almost smiled at the thought.

"Here? You think it might be here?" Leslie's eyes narrowed in doubt.

They had arrived at the Flocking Valley.

Ato ran ahead. "Come help me," he called back. His three friends followed him along the third and final row of flat stone slabs that made up the seats of the Flocking Valley.

Ato stopped a little way past the middle seat. "Look."

"What . . . ?" Hafsat began. "Oh!" she exclaimed, staring at the etching on the stone seat—a pair of falcons, perched on a mountain.

The words of his father's letter rang in his mind.

"Below this rock peak, where the sunlight first greets Nnoma," he whispered. He pointed to the Dawn Locus, rising above them. "Where the falcons watch over the valley."

"So where's the plan?" Dzifa asked breathlessly.

Ato went on his knees and ran exploring fingers beneath the base of the stone seat. His heart quickened. There was an indent, a groove where the flat stone slab had been wedged into the rock beneath it.

"The Jolly Jays," he said, looking up at his team's surprised faces. "Remember one of them trapped their fingers underneath their seat! So these slabs we sat on could move. It only hit me when we were going to give Nana's medicine to Eyra."

He tried to lift it, but the seat did not budge. Peering under the seat, he saw a seal of dirt, caked to concrete by water and sunshine.

"Help me," Ato said to his friends.

Leslie took a step back. "Ato, that's a perfect hideout for scorpions! This thing probably hasn't been moved since Moses lifted *his* tablets."

"Exactly, Leslie." Ato's breathing was short and rapid.

Together, teeth gritted, the Gallant Geese strained to lift the square slab. It shifted. Slowly, ever so slowly, they loosened it and lifted it from the rock beneath.

Ato gave a small cry. There, in a stone hollow beneath the seat, protected from sun, rain, dust, and wind, was a clay pot. It was small enough to fit in his cupped hand, like a mini-teapot without a handle. A knobbed lid fit snugly onto it.

The Gallant Geese stared, silent in amazement.

"Wooooow," Leslie breathed. "It's really here!"

Ato picked up the pot tenderly, cradling it in his hands. He pinched the knob. The top creaked off. Nestled within it was an envelope woven from thick raffia. He opened it and drew out a yellowed folded sheet of paper.

To my son, Ato Turkson

At the sight of his father's bold, slanted handwriting, he sank down onto the nearest seat. He had found the plan!

His friends crowded around him, their heavy breathing like a distant wind. Everything else seemed far, far away. He unfolded the full sheet of paper. Apart from the brown age spots, the letter was in perfect condition.

They read together:

Ato, this place has taken several years to build. The plan for Nnoma is beautiful. The children who come to Nnoma will be like birds; they will migrate all around the world. Wherever they go, like birds, they will drop seeds, seeds of the understanding of how to look after our planet. Nnoma will be a breeding ground for people who will truly love and care for the world. But not everyone wants Nnoma to be used for this.

I have heard whispers, my son. And I sense Nnoma may one day be in danger. People see this place and they see only the gold that is hidden here. How can we protect Nnoma? It is simple.

In the animal world, feathered predators sometimes lurk, concealed or camouflaged, among other birds. These predators want to attack nests and carry off the fledglings. But there's one thing about parents of fledglings; they don't back off easily. True, they could simply fly away. But the instinct to survive as a group is strong, and the species can only survive if the young ones survive. So I have seen what birds do when their young are in danger. One or two birds set up an alarm. A chorus. A call. Other birds hear, and they gather, from everywhere. Then they attack the predator. I see gulls attack carrion crows, and crows and jays and blackbirds attacking eagles and hawks.

If we find a predator in our midst in Nnoma, and see

that younger Asafo are under threat, then this is what we can do too. With enough Asafo from all around the world, we can raise the alarm! We can scare the intruders away. If we make enough noise, the whole world will hear us and stand for us too. The world will protect us. Then young Asafo can keep growing up and going out to be protectors of the world.

Ato looked up. Three astounded faces looked back.

Dzifa raised shaky fists to her chin. "That's exactly what happened! You did it, Ato."

His father had been right, Ato thought, the sheet of paper resting on his lap. Just as he'd told Eyra all those years ago, the directions on what to do were with him all along. Not written in ink. But inside—stamped on his heart.

"We did it," he said, his voice low, grateful. He touched the paper that rested on his lap. "We did it. All of Flock Eleven. And all the Asafo too."

He shut his eyes, feeling the setting sun's warmth stroke his eyelids. *With enough Asafo*, his father had written. And there had been enough of them.

"Thank you," he whispered.

CHAPTER THIRTY-FIVE

IT WAS THE SEVENTH AND LAST DAY ON NNOMA. ATO STOOD on the sun-soaked balcony of the Chirp and Chatter with a phone to his ear. In the distance, the lake reflected the blue sky. Branches in the woods below swayed to a light wind, seeming to wave goodbye.

Below him, Flock Eleven gathered at the Flocking Valley, a moving field of blue and green. The air rang with the excitement of their last-day chatter. Was this how birds felt, getting ready to fly home from migration grounds? he wondered.

He glanced back at the square clock above Clara's head: seven minutes to eleven. In a few minutes, he would need to go down for the Pledge and Badge Ceremony. It was clear that the Gallant Geese were out of the running for the top three. He felt a pang of regret at the thought, but far greater than missing the top three spots was his worry about Eyra and Kai.

How were they? he wondered for the thousandth time. Would he ever see Eyra again? He felt unbearable sadness at the thought that she would not be at the final Asafo ceremony, and that he might not see her again.

He wondered who the new Asafo would be. The Guardians would probably total up final marks based on how much of Mission Eight the teams had been able to complete. After that, they would have lunch, and then pack out of the cabins that had been their homes for the last seven days.

His call went unanswered. He pressed dial again, noticing that Clara had lowered the volume of her TV. Her ear was trained toward him. After yesterday's events, he wasn't surprised she was interested in his phone calls.

"Hello!"

"Max!"

"Hey! The undercover agent of the century! Ato, talk to me. I can't believe you went and found some shady business on Nnoma. But good on you! And on Dzifa. And Mama's Boy."

Ato chuckled at the reference to Leslie. "Max, you were amazing!" he said.

"I had to think fast, kiddo. After your call, I was dead-worried. I could be laying it all on the line here, I thought. My reputation, my career, everything I'd worked for. If it had been fake news, I'd have been ordered away from investigative reporting and dumped in a news backroom for one year to write boring reports. But that guy who called, Richie—there was something too calm about him. My gut told me something wasn't right. Would've had sleepless nights if I hadn't made that move for you."

"Thank you, Max!" Ato beamed.

"Welcome, kiddo. I've been a reporter for years; just when I think nothing can surprise me, something does. Hafsat was right. I spoke to her dad in the prison. He had bags of info. Guess what? Our old friend, Yakayaka, Prophet of Fire . . . ?"

Ato held his breath. "What about him?"

"He comes from the lands around this lake. That's how he knows Richie! And about the gold in the mountain."

"No way!"

"Yup. He and Richie have been talking. For years. When he went to prison, they decided to make a move. The two of them planned this!"

Ato shuddered. "The Prophet is like an octopus, with tentacles everywhere."

"He tried to deny it, but the police said Richie has confessed to putting the poison in Eyra's dawn tonic. And has admitted the Prophet is his accomplice.

"Hafsat's dad has also told police about conversations he'd heard. The Prophet saying stuff about being great again and being richer than ever before. And a *lot* more. Seems like Yakayaka thought Hafsat's dad would be like them, into the money. But Hafsat's dad knew what a beautiful island Nnoma was, and he was happy to stop the Prophet. I think his testimony will get him out earlier. Hafsat is soon going to be a very happy girl!"

"Yes!" Ato exclaimed.

"Now, I know you gotta go soon. Eyra is on everyone's mind. And Kai. Your grandmother did her best. So did all of you. Now let's stay hopeful." He paused. "You know, I gotta get this stuff out on TV. People need to be warned about dirty business like this. I know Eyra is super-private, but if she does get better, I'm gonna do my best to get an interview with her. She closed Nnoma for five years because she was trying to protect the island. Best way to protect Nnoma is make some noise about it, to let the gold diggers know the whole world is on the watch. And your nana too. Awesome woman. I know we're not sure how her medicine has worked for Eyra, but I'm gonna get her to share some of her wisdom in an interview."

He paused. His tone softened. "And Ato. I should thank you."

"What for, Max?"

"'Cos sometimes I forget why I do what I do. Stuff like yesterday helps me remember it's not just about getting hot news out. It's about making a difference in the world—a good difference. Pushing for what's good for everyone. After all, we're all on this big ball together."

Clara's voice piped up. "Ato! Pledge and Badge starting soon. You've got to go."

"'Bye kiddo. See ya when you get back!"

"'Bye, Max!"

Ato walked out into the bright sunshine. What if Max hadn't believed him? Nnoma and everything on it would have been destroyed for a few people to get rich.

Down at the Flocking Valley, he took his place beside his teammates. All sixty-four members of Flock Eleven were seated. Facing them, up on the platform, were the ten Guardians who had been on Eyra's side. The mood was solemn. Richie and his accomplices had turned out to be enemies of Nnoma. Eyra and Kai had been gone since yesterday and no one knew how they were doing.

Suddenly, behind them the quiet was ripped by a cry. Everyone whirled around.

It was Marko! He was standing on the hillside above them, facing them. Ato's stomach constricted. What had happened?

In consternation, all the children in Flock Eleven rose from their seats. The Guardians on the platform looked apprehensive.

"Madam Eyra!" Marko yelled. "She . . ."

"No," Ato breathed, fearing the worst.

Beside him, Dzifa gasped. "Eyra! She's baaaack," she shrieked in disbelief, interrupting the overjoyed cook.

"Wh . . . what?" Ato stuttered.

Dzifa was right. Framed against the trees, a beloved silhouette had appeared at the top of the hill. She sailed down the grassy slope toward them, her blue gown floating behind her in the breeze. A floral scarf was wrapped around her head, like a turban of turquoise flowers. And Kai was with her, walking closely in step behind Eyra.

Whoops erupted from the Flocking Valley. Flock Eleven broke ranks and flew over to her. Even the Guardians tossed aside decorum, hopped off the platform, and darted to their beloved leader.

As the rush of joyful children reached Eyra, she did a hop-cross-skip step. Flock Eleven erupted in elation. Eyra was back, and livelier than ever! Ato was ecstatic to see Kai's bulging eyes rolling watchfully over Flock Eleven.

Ato could not get close to Eyra. But Marko had rushed down too and was a few feet from Ato, groping through the melee of children.

"Marko!" Ato called, forcing his way through the children to the man.

"Ato!" The cook grasped Ato's shoulder. "Madam Eyra have come back."

Ato was astonished to see the hard-faced cook's mouth wobble.

"She has, Marko, she has," Ato whispered, choked with emotion. "Does she remember anything?"

"Yes! Your nana medicine, it make her remember everything! And everybody! Everything that Richie do. No holes in her mind! Doctor say Nana medicine be very good. De deep sleep make Eyra mind repair all de damage. I hear yesterday, de doctors give Nana medicine to Kai too! Kai too remember everything: she say she wan' smack Richie face."

Eyra was making her way through the cheering children, hugging them, and answering them excitedly. When she reached Ato, she embraced him.

"Ato! Nnoma and I will be always grateful to you!" She took his hand and tugged him away gently from the crowd. "There's still time. Come. Let's have a moment."

Ato felt every eye following them as he walked beside Eyra coming to a stop a few feet away from the Flocking Valley. Be' them, the Guardians started up a song with Flock Ele' slipped her arm around his shoulder and stood looking out toward the lake.

"Ato, this is exactly where your father and I sat talking, all those years ago. We had been excited about all the young people who would come here." Her hold around his shoulder tightened and she turned her dark eyes to him. "Then your father turned serious. 'Money changes everything, Eyra,' he said to me. 'Nnoma, and this dream we have for children, is in danger of being betrayed for money.'"

Her eyes clouded over. "I was confused, Ato. I told your father I would never kill a dream as beautiful as this for something as common as money.

"'You wouldn't, Eyra,' he said. 'But others will. When you've always had money, you can call it common.'"

"I became angry. Nnoma is mine, I told your father. I told him I wouldn't allow enemies of this dream to step on this island. Then he said something that scared me for a long time. He said, 'Aboa bi beka wo a na ofiri wo ntoma mu.'" Eyra gave him a questioning look. "Ato, do you know what that means?"

He did. "A bug that means to bite you will hide inside your clothing," he replied.

She nodded. "And this is exactly what happened. I heard whispers about people who somehow had heard of Nnoma's treasure, and wanted to get to it. I became increasingly suspicious of people, scared about everything. Eventually my fear made me close Nnoma. It was supposed to be for just six months. Months turned to years. I let go of many old staff and only kept the ones

I trusted most. They stayed on even with no kids coming. They were loyal to me, and faithful to the dream. Or so I thought." She turned her gaze back toward the lake and smiled. "Courage finally replaced my fear, and I opened Nnoma again."

"I'm glad you were brave and opened it, Eyra," Ato said. He slipped his hand through hers and squeezed hard.

She squeezed his hand back and smiled. "So am I, Ato. Your father told me that you would be a protector of our world. And wherever he is, I'm sure he's proud of you." She gave a deep, contented sigh. "Come now," she said, pulling him back toward the Flocking Valley. "The moment we have been waiting for."

Eyra quickly walked to the platform and stood with the eleven Guardians, facing the children.

"Flock Eleven." She beamed. "It is time for you to head back to your homes. You have all grown and have learned a lot since you got here. From now on, wherever you go, the world will be different because you are there." She nodded to Kai.

"Now let us welcome our Asafo!" Kai announced. Her high-pitched screech was sweetly comforting to Ato. "After adding up all the marks from all seven and a half missions, these are our winners from third to first: ALL SIXTEEN TEAMS!"

Flock Eleven sat in stunned silence. Gasps of astonishment rose. Then rapturous applause broke out.

Eyra, Kai, and the rest of the Guardians clapped along, eyes shining with pleasure.

Eyra raised her arms to quiet them down. "You are all A
she declared. "Brave young people who love and unde'

earth. You spoke truth to power and stood for what was right even when bigger people tried to stop you. You would not let anyone stand in your way. And that is how we select Asafo. It's not just about points, or about what you are called; it's who you are inside!"

Another cheer erupted from the elated children. Ato closed his eyes, dizzy with elation. Kai and the Guardians were beckoning them forward. Like a sleepwalker he rose to his feet. On either side of him, Hafsat, Dzifa, and Leslie took turns hugging and high-fiving each other, jumping and skipping in their euphoria.

One by one, the new Asafo mounted the Flock Rock. Eyra handed each one a small box before they returned to their seats.

"Open your boxes," Kai instructed.

With fumbling fingers, Ato opened his box . . . and gasped.

A black-and-silver badge, etched with four geese in the classic arrowhead flight formation, lay gleaming on a square of dark velvet.

Eyra clasped her hands before her. "In twenty-four hours the Gallant Geese pulled a victory almost too amazing to fathom. In honor of this courageous team, these badges, expressly sent in by Asafo out in the world, bear the images of geese. This will become the official emblem of the Asafo. Whenever we see these magnificent birds high up in flight, let's remember that if we stick together and work together, we can save the world together!"

This time the cheers from Flock Eleven were so loud, alarmed birds flapped into the air from the surrounding trees, squawking their outrage.

Trembling with pride, Ato slid the sleek pin through his T-shirt. He raised his head and made direct eye contact with Bello.

Bello touched his fingers to his forehead in salute. Congratulations, he mouthed. With a smile of respect, Ato returned the gesture.

Guardians quickly handed out brown cards headed with the words *Asafo Pledge* in cursive black font.

The warm, still air resounded with the unified voices of the Asafo, strong with hope:

I am an Asafo, and today I do make
A solemn promise for Mother Earth's sake:
In all my ways I will love and respect her
And fearlessly do what is best to protect her.
I'll protect her forests, plains, deserts, and mountains,
Her valleys, air, rivers, oceans, and fountains.
On land, below land, and up in the sky,
Protect creatures that crawl, run, swim, leap, and fly.
Humankind dwelling in lands far and near,
I pledge to honor each one's right to be here.
By thought, word, and action I'll be a pacesetter
And leave in my trail a place not worse—but better.

Above Ato, the golden sun hovered above the Dawn Locus, radiating light in every direction. Silhouetted against it soared a falcon, scanning the earth. It was looking for its target, Ato thought. Its instructions were written on its heart. In time, it would find it.

ACKNOWLEDGMENTS

This journey to the island of Nnoma was achieved with the help of several key people:

My super-agent Sarah. In her capable hands, this dream has come true.

My skillful editor Helen Thomas, who helps me view possibilities beyond my horizon.

Kristin Allard—kindness, ability, and helpfulness personified.

The entire team at Norton Young Readers.

My alpha readers—my husband Rami, and children Alia, Rami, and Rima. You never fail me . . . even at the eleventh hour.

My father Anthony Sackey, for the endless supply of books in my childhood and the endless encouragement even in adulthood.

My Sackey, Baitie, and Kofi clan for their unfailing support. Family rocks!

And to the Creator of all islands and worlds . . .

Thank you!

ABOUT THE AUTHOR

Elizabeth-Irene Baitie says, "Even as a young child, I was a voracious reader. By the age of seven, my dream was to create stories that would captivate young people just the same way the books I had read did." She studied biochemistry with chemistry at the University of Ghana and earned an MSc in clinical biochemistry and molecular biology at the University of Surrey in Britain, before founding and directing a medical laboratory in Ghana. "The writer in me wasn't pickled in the chemistry lab, though," she adds. Her first novel, *A Saint in Brown Sandals*, won the Macmillan Writer's Prize for Africa. Subsequent books include *The Twelfth Heart*, winner of the Burt Award for African Literature; *Rattling in the Closet*; *The Lion's Whisper*, which was a finalist for the Burt Award for African Young Adult Literature; and, most recently, *Crossing the Stream*, which was named as an Honor Book for the Children's Africana Book Award. Elizabeth-Irene lives in Accra with her husband. They have three adult children.